The Extraordinary Adventures of Endingen Mole

Steve Ferrett

ISBN: 1502334380
ISBN 13: 9781502334381
Library of Congress Control Number: 2014918981
CreateSpace Independent Publishing Platform
North Charleston, South Carolina

To my Kay – You are my tower of strength

To Bethan – Follow your dreams and
keep writing – Love, Bumplecheese

To Dave, David and Matthew – Sadly
departed but always in my heart

Table of Contents

Chapter I

A Mole's Life

It is very difficult to tell the story of a creature when he doesn't have a name. Well, at least he doesn't know his real name just yet. So for now, we shall refer to him by using the name of the village he lives in.

Introducing little Endingen Mole. His address, according to himself and for the benefit of the postman, is:

Endingen Mole
Number 1,
A Small Hole
Beneath the Ground
In a Field
Near a Wood

Endingen Mole was an orphan. Despite not knowing the meaning of the word "orphan," he knew that he had no family to share his life with. This made him very sad at times, but also quite inquisitive, meaning he felt the need to ask lots of questions. This behavior was considered very "un-mole-like," at least according to Madame Victoria, his matriarch and adviser on mole life.

The madame was a large, round lady mole with a stern expression. As she constantly reminded him, it was her job to ensure that he became proficient in the ways of a mole. In particular, she advised the use of daily checklists for keeping his life in order and, above all, efficient.

When Madame Victoria left Endingen on his own, he didn't particularly miss her company. But, whether he liked it or not, checklists had become a major part of his life.

> Who am I? I am a mole, just an ordinary mole. *Check.*
> Where do I live? In a mole hole, an ordinary hole. *Check.*
> What are today's tasks?
>
> > Catch some worms. *Check.*
> > Eat lunch. *Check.*
> > Clean lavatory tunnel section. *Oh, dear. Yuck. Oh, OK. Check.*
> > Dig new tunnel in a north-northeasterly direction (have compass at the ready). *Check.*
> > Store leftover worms in the larder as stock for the winter. *Check.*

This was Endingen Mole's standard daily checklist, which he completed day in and day out in a very orderly and highly efficient manner.

"Nothing out of the ordinary today," he thought as he went about his daily business. Every day seemed so ordinary to Endingen; he wished that one day something extraordinary would happen to him.

Chapter 2

An Unexpected Discovery

Endingen Mole let out a huge yawn after gorging himself on a large pile of delicious earthworms for his lunch. He had nearly completed all of his daily chores as per his checklist, the last one being to store all of his leftover worms in the larder room.

The earth felt cold and damp, a sure sign that a harsh winter was nearly upon him, so a stockpile of food was essential to survive the coming months. Endingen Mole had a very healthy appetite, and so the more food he stored, the better.

Storage cupboards adorned the room; they were entirely overloaded with mountains of delicious worms. In the corner of the larder room stood a large, dusty old cupboard, pitted heavily with woodworm holes. It leaned precariously to one side and had definitely seen better days, but it was the only one with any space left.

"Right," thought Endingen Mole, "let's store this pile of worms and then retire for a well-earned sleep."

As he loaded the last of the worms into the drawers in a rather slapdash manner, the old cupboard suddenly shook violently, moved abruptly backward, and then came crashing down onto the floor with an incredibly loud BANG!

Worms, dust, and fragments of rotten wood were everywhere.

"Oh, what a right old mess!" cried Endingen Mole. "This wasn't expected, or on my checklist!"

After the dust had settled, and the remaining worms had wriggled off back into the walls of the tunnel, Endingen Mole knew he had to decide what to do next. This was very strange to him. Making decisions was something that had never been mentioned by Madame Victoria, and it was definitely not an item on his checklist.

"OK," he muttered, "that's it for the day. I will add the cleanup operation to my checklist for tomorrow."

With that, he was about to scuttle off down the tunnel when, through the debris, he noticed something hanging on the wall where the cupboard once stood.

As you know, moles have very poor eyesight and require extremely powerful glasses. Therefore, as he approached the wall, he put on his reading glasses and squinted at what turned out to be a dusty old picture frame. Within the frame was a parchment drawing with several small, mole-like figures scattered across what appeared to be a map of somewhere. The more he studied it, the more it became strangely familiar to him.

He wiped away the patches of dust with his soft, leathery paws and read aloud the words that appeared at the top. "The whereabouts of very special local moles and other friendly creatures."

He realized that he was perhaps not alone, and that there were many interesting creatures locally, so he decided to make a new checklist, an adventure checklist. His thoughts turned to exciting adventures travelling to meet these "very special local moles and other friendly creatures." He intended to ask them many interesting questions.

He began to wonder if Madame Victoria would approve. "I don't think she *would* approve of such behavior," he said, chuckling to himself. "I want to know everything, but first, some sleep. I'm utterly exhausted," he said with a huge yawn.

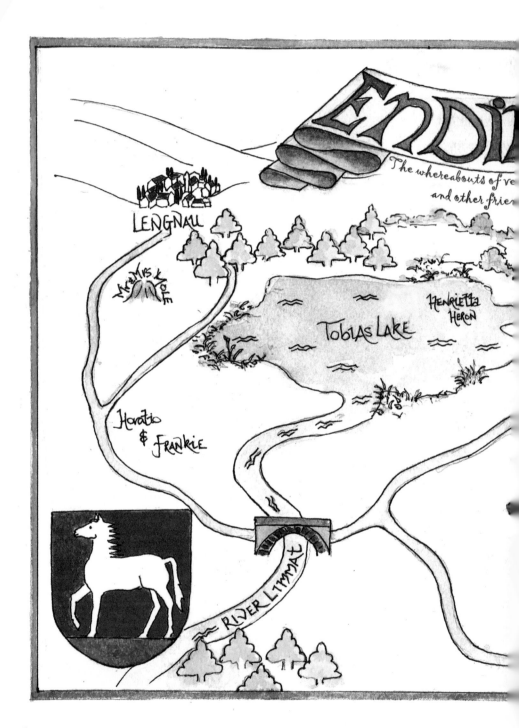

Chapter 3

The Adventure Checklist

Following a good night's sleep, Endingen Mole awoke in a particularly determined mood. His usual thoughts pertaining to his boring daily tasks were clearly not his utmost priority on this day. Instead, he spent at least four hours studying the map. "I've got to decide exactly who I'm going to visit, and which way I'll go," he thought.

Given the huge travelling distances required, this was no easy task. Taking one's time was of the utmost importance. Some of the creatures on the map resided as far as ten mole miles away, a distance Endingen could not quite imagine.

One name and address stood out and excited young Endingen. "Mr. and Mrs. A. and E. Molesworthy of Lengnau," he recited over and over again. These folks were referred to as an interesting couple, which appealed to Endingen. They were bound to have a large selection of tasty foods available. And he would need a considerable amount of rest and food to recuperate following his monumental journey. The thought of scrumptious, home-cooked dishes served in comfortable surroundings made his tummy grumble as lunchtime approached.

Following an enjoyable lunch and a brief snooze, he decided to consider visiting other interesting nonmole folk that were marked on the map. Field mice, toads, and even bats appeared, along with a hedgehog, shrew, and heron.

Some of the creatures were similar to moles, though not necessarily in the way they looked. Rather, these creatures lived their lives like moles, burrowing in tunnels, searching for food, and living a mostly solitary life.

Madame Victoria had mentioned that it was OK to say hello to these creatures, but no more. She had also said that by far, moles were superior creatures in all other aspects. Endingen was confused by all of this talk of superiority and decided he would make up his own mind. He was his own mole and would form his own opinions.

Some of the other creatures were unfamiliar to Endingen. He had never seen any of them before, having only read about them in his nature encyclopedias. "Wow," he thought. "It would be very interesting to meet and spend some time with these creatures."

Finally, after he had spent another few hours studying his map, a satisfied smile spread across Endingen's face, from one set of whiskers to the other. He had finally finished his adventure checklist and decided to read it aloud.

> Adventure checklist
> Adventure number-one, priority destination determined:
> *Check. (Mr. and Mrs. A. and E. Molesworthy of Lengnau.)*
> Distance to interesting local mole couple calculated: 6.5
> mole miles. *Check.*
> Route to destination plotted on map. *Check.*
> Underground tunnel or overground scramble travel decision made. *Ah, um, oh dear. NOT checked.*

This was a major problem for Endingen, and a setback for his adventurous journey plan. "How can I travel to where I want to get to, and do it safely at the same time?" he thought.

Option one: "I've tunnelled underground every single day of my life." He calculated that it would take three weeks to reach his destination that way.

Option two: "I'm not good at scrambling above ground," he thought. "Though this would be much quicker, and the journey would take just a few days"—he shuddered—"if all went well."

Endingen knew only too well that this form of travel—namely "UP THERE," as Madame Victoria referred to it—would be fraught with danger. Never having practiced this form of travel, Endingen felt a sense of foreboding in his heart at the idea.

"No time to waste," a determined young Endingen thought. "I must make a decision soon and then start planning the journey checklist."

"Underground or above ground?" occupied his thoughts all night. Over and over and over it churned in his mind. He kept rolling around in his bed trying to sleep, but the decision had to be made. Then he could relax.

Suddenly, he stood bolt upright and shouted at the top of his voice, "I have decided! I have a plan!" Then he muttered, "I hope I've made the right choice," before finally drifting off into a very deep sleep.

Chapter 4

The Journey Begins

"**A**bove ground!" cried Endingen as he sped through his tunnel complex the next morning. This was a dramatic start to the new day, and he continued to shout out his plan over and over again as he rushed to make all of the necessary arrangements. He had now decided exactly how he would travel on his journey.

"Now I just need to compile my journey checklist before I depart on my adventure," he thought. He had, however, another major worry that occupied his mind during breakfast. Other than the briefest educational discussions with Madame Victoria on the subject, in which she lectured him on mole etiquette and behavior, Endingen knew very little about other creatures.

To his credit, he had been studying this vast subject daily, his head almost always buried in a nature book or encyclopedia. But this gave him absolutely no idea of how he should interact with these creatures should there be an encounter.

What would his first words be? *Hi? Hello? Who are you and what do you want?* Or maybe: *hang on—you're not a mole, are you?* And what if things went wrong? He was sure that not all creatures would be friendly.

No checklist could ever prepare him for an encounter with another creature. While musing over these questions, he decided that it was best just to be himself. Luckily, from what we have seen so far, little Endingen Mole had many good qualities. He was thoughtful, bright, inquisitive, good natured, and generally quite humorous.

Therefore, if and when he met another creature, he planned to introduce himself politely, offer the creature a choice of various foods, and engage the creature in a friendly conversation. "Yes, friendly," he thought. "Or so I hope." Endingen sighed, wiped the lenses of his glasses, and then gathered up his checklist.

> Journey checklist
> Map and compass. *Check.*
> Backpack loaded with various foodstuffs and supplies. *Check.*
> Exit point from tunnel to overground molehill identified. *Check.*
> Feel happy to leave the comfort of my lovely home and go on the adventure of a lifetime. *Ah, ah, oh, oh dear. Check.*

"Of course I am happy to leave the comfort of my lovely home, aren't I?" he thought. With his journey checklist finally complete and spoken aloud, albeit rather unconvincingly, Endingen mole was ready to embark on his life-changing adventure.

His sharp claws dug into the cold, dark, musty-smelling soil, and after a few short thrusts, he felt painfully bright rays of sunshine through his squinting eyes. He stood up. An icy blast of wind chilled his bones. He felt dizzy. "It must be that I'm not used to the amount of air outside of my tunnel," he thought.

He had, however, made up his mind. He wanted to meet all of the new creatures marked on the map and knew this was the only way. But this was a very strange and unfamiliar—and potentially very dangerous—place for such a young and inexperienced mole to travel.

He had come this far. He looked back at his tunnel and smiled as he whispered to himself, "It is time for me to start my adventure."

Chapter 5

Danger and Rescue

"Ceeaww! Ceeaww!"

This haunting cry filled the air. Little Endingen was fearful, and he scurried about, racing from one hiding spot to another.

"Ceeaww! Ceeaww!"

Endingen peered up to see what creature was making the terrifying sounds. He saw a large, red kite circling high above the thin clouds. Endingen knew this bird was hunting for its prey. It circled around and around, watching and waiting to spot the movement of a creature below. A slow creature such as a mole travelling above ground would be easy pickings for this deadly hunter.

Endingen scrambled into some long grass and lay close to the ground. His breath slowed. He was lying as frozen as a statue. He listened as the "Ceeaww" sounds continued above. He heard more and more calls as the voices echoed in all directions. "Oh no," he thought, "now there are more than one on the hunt."

After what seemed to be an eternity, the kites' hunting calls faded into the distance. Endingen sighed. He was beginning to seriously regret his decision to travel above ground.

By now Endingen was feeling tired. He decided to have a quick snack and a short rest before he continued on his journey. He missed the safety and comfort of his home but knew that he was destined to start this journey, and he was determined to continue.

After a time, he was clear of the long grass and had made what he believed was good progress. Suddenly, he heard a deep rumbling sound in the distance. The soil around him trembled, and the deep rumbles closed in from all directions.

He wiped his glasses and squinted into the distance. An enormous black shadow appeared. It grew bigger and bigger. The noise was now deafening, and the ground beneath him shook. Endingen recognized the sound and the unmistakeable shape of a plowing machine.

He started to dart around, forward and then backward, left and then right, shrieking loudly, "There is no escape. I am doomed!"

He knew these machines had churned up many mole tunnels in the past, especially ones built too close to the surface, and now it was heading ever closer to him. "This is the end of my adventure, before it has even started," he thought.

Frozen with fear, he lay on the ground. His paws gripped the loose soil, and he closed his eyes.

BANG! Something hit him in his side. He felt himself tumbling through the air, his glasses flying off the end of his nose.

"I have you," exclaimed a high-pitched voice. "Hold on!"

The air rushed through Endingen's fur as he was thrown left and then right at tremendous speed. He was travelling so fast he could hardly take a breath. As he glanced down, he saw two fuzzy shapes that he thought were enormous ears. He soon realized that he was hanging precariously on the back of a huge, brown hare.

"You, my friend, are one very lucky little mole," said the hare as they fled into the safety of a forest. "What on earth were you thinking, being above ground? Aren't moles supposed to be underground? There are real dangers here, so many dangers. Has no one ever explained that to you?"

Endingen shook his head mournfully and muttered, "Well, actually, no, they haven't."

The hare handed Endingen's glasses to him, shaking his head. "Alone, directionless, and blind. I am Harold," he announced, "or as my many friends call me, Hopping Harold, the hare in a hurry." Harold jumped and circled Endingen twice. "Whatever you are doing and wherever you are going is of no concern to me, but take my advice—travel only at night and below ground if you can."

Endingen listened to Harold and nodded in agreement. Perhaps he was right. "However can I repay you, Harold?" asked Endingen. "Please share some of my food. I have juicy worms, bugs, and some nuts, if you prefer."

Harold stood still in front of Endingen. "Thanks, but no thanks. I am a vegetarian and only eat grass. And anyhow, I am in a hurry."

Endingen opened his mouth to speak, but Harold keep talking in his fast, high-pitched voice. "Now, listen to my advice carefully. It would be best for you to quickly burrow back into that molehill of yours and return to wherever your underground home is."

"OK," started Endingen, "but I—"

"Good!" shouted Harold. "I've got to run. Stay safe, little mole!" With that—and a shake of his bushy, white tail—Harold bounded off like the wind.

Endingen sat and considered Harold's words and reflected on the events of the day. Traveling above ground on his own was far too dangerous. He decided that, although it would take a much longer time, the best way of traveling was underground. He was determined that he would dig and dig until he got to where he was meant to go.

He made his way slowly back to the entrance of his tunnel and burrowed down. The familiar damp smell and dim light made young Endingen feel very happy and, more importantly, safe. He reflected for a short time on what had happened and knew that he had to plan his journey far better. He decided to do this slowly, surely, and safely—underground.

One thing that moles are very good at is tunnelling. He thrust his head forward, and his paws quickly started to remove the soil in front of him.

Chapter 6

End of the Tunnel

Three weeks, four days, and six hours later, twenty-six large candles used, and food supplies reaching critically low levels, Endingen Mole sighed. He was not in a particularly good mood for a number of reasons.

He had estimated that this whole underground tunnelling adventure should have only taken two weeks. Unfortunately, calculating such a complex journey was not his strong point. Half of the journey was spent checking his directions on the map, aided only by a very old compass and illuminated only by candlelight and, of course, his mole senses. The other major activities that had distracted him from his mission were, of course, his two favorite pastimes: eating huge amounts of food and sleeping.

He was, however, very close to where he estimated his first port of call should be—the residence of Mr. and Mrs. A. and E. Molesworthy of Lengnau. It was time to burrow upward now and see how well he had managed with his navigation and map-reading skills. Deep down inside, Endingen was not too confident.

He used all his might to push upward while pulling the dark, heavy soil underneath his body. Suddenly, a cool blast of night air poured into the hole. He had arrived at his destination. Filled with a huge sense of pride and achievement, he set off to explore.

Chapter 7

The Brotherhood of Bats

The tree was large, with huge branches that were long and thin and that appeared very spiky; set against the bright moon and clear, star-filled sky, they painted a haunting and eerie image. From a distance there seemed to be lots of dark shapes suspended from the branches. As he watched closely, Endingen noticed the shapes had started to move.

One eye, two eyes, a pair, another pair, and yet another. Eyes opening everywhere. Within what seemed a matter of seconds, hundreds, maybe even thousands, of eyes had opened and were staring straight at the startled mole.

Endingen could not believe what he was seeing; the whole tree was a sea of dark-winged bodies with piercingly bright, orange eyes. Then, from nowhere, came a shrill cry in unison that pierced the silent night air and echoed over and over again.

"We are the Brotherhood of Bats. Come closer. Join us. Be one of us."

For once, Endingen was speechless and very shocked, but he managed a stuttering reply. "I am a mole from Endingen, and I am on an adventure. I would like to meet the very interesting folk drawn on this map. I am traveling by myself but need help in finding my way. If you help me, I will offer you some of the delicious food that I have in my backpack. Can you help me, please?" he inquired confidently.

Bright eyes blinked rapidly, and then the echoing voices fell silent. Suddenly, a much larger, darker figure, hanging upside down, started to move very quickly from side to side at the top of the tree. Its wings started to unfold and soon were completely outstretched, blocking the bright moonlight. The wings slowly started to beat with a deep, whooshing sound. The figure moved high into the night sky. The formidable shape then glided silently downward and landed gracefully next to the little mole.

The creature's huge body and enormous wings, even when folded, made Endingen feel very nervous. With a deep and menacing voice, the creature introduced himself. "I am Boris, leader and voice of the Brotherhood of Bats."

His huge wings, when completely unfolded, were at least three times as long as the tiny mole and were a truly awe-inspiring sight. Against the moonlight, the leathery wings revealed long, pulsing, deep-red veins. Large, sharp-looking talons adorned the tops and ends of each wing.

Soon the outstretched wings started to move toward Endingen, and within seconds they had completely covered him; there was now no light and very little air to breathe. Endingen's head was firmly pressed against the warm, fur-covered body of the huge bat, and he could clearly hear the deep echo of the creature's booming heartbeat.

"We very much want what you have offered, and we need to feed. The Brotherhood will take it. Now come, brother Endingen, join us—be one of us."

Endingen had never seen a bat before, let alone been completely engulfed by one. Very soon, he started to think of the bats he had read about in his encyclopedia. Vivid and scary images of vampire bats who fed on their victims' blood filled his thoughts. Endingen started to panic, and he pushed and struggled, trying to break free of the giant bat's grip.

The thought of becoming a late-night meal for these bats made him shake nervously and his heart race. He was being held so tightly that his muffled, merciful plea took most of his breath away. "Please, please, brother Boris, I am an orphaned mole who seeks the friendship of others—please don't take my blood."

The large wings unfolded immediately, and the cold air filled Endingen's breathless lungs. He heard a chorus of what sounded like laughing coming from the tree, and then silence fell again. As he looked toward the huge bat, Boris spoke clearly. "My dear Endingen Mole, I feel ashamed that you thought my affectionate embrace was in any way sinister. This is simply how I and my clan of brothers greet new friends. The Brotherhood of Bats accepts you as our brother."

He further explained, to Endingen's considerable relief, that the brotherhood was made up of very sociable, insect-eating bats who had nothing in common with their solitary and infamous vampire cousins. "Come brothers, come," Boris encouraged the others. "Embrace our new friend and feed on the wonderful bounty he has so kindly offered us."

The bats squeaked loudly and shrilly and swooped to the ground, excited by the sight of the feast that Endingen was offering. Insects of all kinds were devoured greedily by hundreds of hungry mouths, and then, yet again, there was silence. Boris moved toward Endingen, and this time the young mole wasn't so afraid of the embrace from the huge bat.

The brotherhood and Endingen talked and talked. Soon, the bats understood exactly who Endingen Mole was and the journey he was on. He showed them the map and explained that he needed to visit Mr. and Mrs. A. and E. Molesworthy of Lengnau.

Boris and many in the brotherhood explained that the area Endingen had burrowed into was full of many, many moles. He would need to speak to a very wise creature that knew the whereabouts of everyone and had insight into everything. The brotherhood agreed to take Endingen to the creature as thanks for his delicious food and wonderful company, and, in particular, as a gesture of their newfound friendship.

The creature he needed to find was called Tobias the Tale-Telling Toad and was located far from where they were. The only way to find him quickly was to travel by air. Endingen was initially extremely worried at the thought of flying. Moles dig and burrow—they don't fly. But soon the fear faded, as he now trusted his new friends.

Before long, he was surrounded by the brotherhood, who grasped and held him very securely with their strong, leathery wings and powerful claws. Endingen looked around him as the brotherhood flapped their wings in unison, and he felt his whole body slowly lift off of the ground.

He gasped, "Simply incredible, truly amazing! What an evening! This is what I call an adventure!"

Chapter 8

No or *Qui?*
Tobias, the Tale-Telling Toad

As the chill winds brushed through and ruffled Endingen's fur at great speed, he began to think very deeply. Two days ago he was covered in wet, peaty mud, tired and wishing that his digging operation would come to an end. He was not sure that this adventure would ever succeed.

Now he was flying—yes, flying—above the countryside, supported by a mass of black, winged bodies. The Brotherhood of Bats, his newfound friends, was taking the little mole's quest to new heights.

As Endingen looked down at the darkness below, the only illumination was the twinkle of distant house lights. He drew a huge, deep breath and sighed contentedly. He was sure that this was the start of an epic adventure, the adventure he had yearned for all of his life.

"Landing very soon," the bats whispered in unison. Soon, they were approaching a very dark wood, blacker and more eerie than the night sky. The flapping of hundreds of pairs of wings slowed, and they gently lowered Endingen onto the moss-covered forest floor. He had arrived safely, now to find the infamous and apparently legendary tale-telling toad called Tobias.

Boris turned to Endingen, and, with a huge, sharp-toothed smile, he announced, "Brother Endingen, you now seek the toad who is very close by. Look for a shining, green lake and you will find him. You will also hear his endless gossiping in the night air. He should be easy to find. But beware," Boris continued, "he will not provide you with the information you require easily. You must find a way of getting it, and getting it quickly. When you are satisfied, and while it is still dark, call us as loudly as you can, and the brotherhood will once again stand by your side. Good luck, brother Mole." The embrace that followed was as warm and heartfelt as usual and made Endingen very happy.

"Bats of the brotherhood—FLY!" boomed Boris. Leaves and twigs flew into the air as the black shapes lifted into the night sky. Within seconds, only a dark silhouette outlined against the moon remained; a moment later, it was gone. Endingen was once again alone.

"Green lake. I need to find a green lake," he said out loud as he scuttled quickly in the direction of the woods. After what seemed like an age and a great distance traveled, Endingen still hadn't found the lake. He stopped and listened.

First there was only silence and the rustle of leaves. Then his heartbeat quickened, as out of the forest came a low, croaky voice making a seemingly endless number of announcements.

"Bats landing and taking off. Strange burrowing creature, not from this area, spotted. Woodpeckers squabbling all day. Strange shrew seen fishing illegally. Ooh, la, la, news, news, hear my news, creatures one and all," the voice continued.

The strange outburst was followed by a huge grumbling and croaking sound that made the nearby ground shake. This surely had to be the tale-telling toad that Endingen had been searching for. He began laughing to himself. How could the news of his arrival be known to this creature when he had been completely shrouded in darkness and his movements were under the cover of dark? This was obviously a truly fascinating creature.

"Hungry, hungry, need my dinner. Hungry, hungry, going to snare my food," squealed the toad. At that exact moment, a huge pink tongue came flying toward Endingen. He was startled and tried to make his escape, but he was nowhere near fast enough.

The whiplike sound was the tongue wrapping itself around Endingen's body and squeezing him very tightly. He flew through the air at great speed and was confronted by a huge, green shape sitting next to a shining, green lake.

Eyes looked into eyes and nose pressed against nose, and yet not a word was said. Both Endingen and the toad continued to look at each other up and down. The very next moment, the toad took a huge breath, and a twinkle appeared in his deep green eyes. He let the huge breath out, and once again Endingen was flying through the air, this time landing unceremoniously in a heap on the riverbank.

"Bonjour, bonjour! You don't look too tasty. A mole, ooh la la, a mole. Yuck, pah. What a disgusting creature!" the toad spluttered.

Endingen wiped off the thick layer of slime that had been deposited on his fur and watched with fascination as the toad began to hop from one side of the riverbank to the other. He was by now getting extremely agitated and croaked, "I know who you are, mole. You have traveled here from across the valley, and you go by the name of Endingen. You are seeking other moles—a certain couple in Lengnau, if I am not mistaken. Many creatures come to me to seek all kinds of information, and I will gladly give it to them on the condition that they pass my test. Do you agree to take the test in return for information?" he asked Endingen.

"Has anyone ever passed your test?" Endingen inquired."

No, no, no, of course not, my little burrowing friend. I have high standards, and I am afraid the creatures come nowhere near giving me the answers I seek," he said, sneering at Endingen.

"I will take your test," agreed Endingen.

"For you to pass the Tobias test, you must answer three questions correctly, showing that you have an intelligent and imaginative mind. Is that clear?" Tobias asked.

Endingen nodded in agreement.

"When you answer a question, I will answer in one of two ways. If your answer is indeed well thought out and it satisfies me, then I will say 'qui,' which means 'yes.' If the answer is not of the standard that I require, then I will simply say 'no.' That 'no' is a very definite 'no,' and you will be asked to leave," Tobias said abruptly.

Endingen nodded and concentrated, listening carefully. He hoped his love of reading and his vivid imagination would help him provide Tobias with the answers he was seeking.

Tobias hopped close to Endingen and croaked very loudly. "First question: take a long, long look at me and tell me what you see."

Endingen thought for a while, remembering what he had read about toads. "I see before me the mightiest of amphibians. Your wonderful warts are large, brown, and extremely slimy."

The toad nodded and paused; he wanted more. Endingen continued, "I see a wise face that understands everything around, a sign of intelligence and charm."

Tobias drew in a huge breath and croaked loudly, "I hear your answer and say"—he paused, smiled, and croaked—"*qui*. Second question: Listen to my voice and tell me what you hear."

Endingen again concentrated and thought very hard before he gave his reply. "Tobias, your impressive voice can be heard for miles around, loudly and clearly. The information you give, and the current affairs you know so well, are both important and valued. You are by far the finest of communicators."

Tobias once again paused and then nodded again. With another great breath, he replied, "I hear your answer and again I say"—he paused, smiled, and croaked again—"*qui*. And my final question, young mole…" he said as small grin appeared. "Look at my lake, the beautiful Tobias lake, and tell me what you feel."

Endingen turned around in a full circle and slowly examined the landscape in more detail as the moonlight illuminated the lake. "I see a deep green glow from the water, and I feel the same glow when I listen to you. I look at the mighty trees with strong branches, and I look at the clear water. I feel that these are like you too—strong and pure. I feel that the lake and you are one, Tobias," he said with great feeling.

Tobias started to smile and hop excitedly from side to side, and as before, he said, "I hear your answer, and for the last time I say *qui, qui, qui*."

Endingen felt relief but also felt very proud of the way he had answered the questions.

"You are indeed a very clever and charming young mole, Endingen," said Tobias. "I will share with you the names of two creatures who are well-known to me. They will guide you to wherever you need to go," he explained. "But, first things first—we must celebrate and share a meal!"

The remaining food Endingen carried in his rucksack was devoured with great delight by Tobias. He was extremely content and was very soon telling Endingen all about the other local inhabitants and the many daily events happening far and wide. He was soon whispering the names of the two creatures that Endingen would need to find in order to find Mr. and Mrs. A. and E. Molesworthy of Lengnau.

The meal was eventually finished, and Tobias looked at Endingen. "Go, go, go, young Endingen. Your friends should come for you now because the morning will be upon us soon."

Endingen shouted at the top of his voice, "Brotherhood of Bats, come!" Minutes passed, and nothing. Over and over again, Endingen shouted in vain.

"My dear Endingen, please stand back," Tobias said in a soothing voice. He drew a huge gasp of air, then croaked a ground-shaking announcement, "Come, bats, your brother needs you!" He then said, "Now, young Endingen, wait and listen to my last words." He put his short arm close to Endingen and in a soft voice said, "if you ever need my wisdom, please ask. You are indeed a brave little mole. It was a great pleasure meeting you, but now I must go." With this, the giant toad winked, waved, and bounded off into a large, green reed bed.

Endingen now knew that he was much closer to finding Mr. and Mrs. Molesworthy, and eagerly awaited his brotherhood of friendly bats. He did not have to wait long. Soon he was being embraced by the familiar figure of Boris. Boris was very impressed that Endingen had passed the toad's test, a feat that no other creature had ever achieved.

Soon Endingen was being held tightly and whisked through the air again. The bats were heading for an area that had many mole tunnels. The landing, as smooth and controlled as usual, happened as the first glimmers of sunlight appeared over the icy-looking hills. Boris and the brotherhood lowered their heads in a salute but said no words. They soon flew off silently to find their roost.

There was no need for words; lasting friendships had been made with both the multitude of bats and a single, enormous, very complicated but very wise, old toad. Endingen clasped his map tightly and burrowed below ground, knowing that after a rest he would be continuing his journey to finally meet Mr. and Mrs. Molesworthy of Lengnau. He was extremely happy and enormously excited.

Chapter 9

Sometimes the Best Things Come in Small Packages

As Endingen started to drift into a deep sleep and his very weary body became relaxed and limp, the crumpled map fell from his grasp onto the floor. Unknown to him, on the reverse side was a very neatly written note. The author was a certain Tobias Toad. It read:

My Dearest Endingen Mole,

It was a very great pleasure meeting you and discussing your adventure, and indeed those you seek to meet. With this in mind, I will shortly instruct a very capable guide to join you. His advice will assist you in navigating your way safely to the residence of the moles in Lengnau.

Oh, just one thing: never question his small stature in any way, or you will receive a series of one-sided lectures. Best of luck.

Your friend,
Tobias

Endingen was sleeping deeply. Dreams came and went, usually regarding eating, sleeping, and flying. He needed this long sleep badly after what seemed to be a whirlwind start to his adventure.

Suddenly, there was a flicker of light in the distance, dim at first but then brighter; it started to illuminate the far end of the tunnel nearest the entrance hole. Something was trying—very noisily—to clamber down into the tunnel without much success.

"Mole, mole, HELP. I'm stuck," screeched an unfamiliar voice. "Come on, mole, get a wiggle on and give me a hand!"

Endingen opened his eyes and squinted in the direction of the light and the shrill voice. He slowly made his way toward the light and was confronted by an extremely strange sight.

A candlestick hung from one tiny, furry paw; a long, thin tail flopped down onto the floor of the tunnel; and two spindly legs flapped uncontrollably in front of his face. He moved closer to investigate the bizarre happenings.

"Hello, can I help in any way?" Endingen politely inquired.

"Don't just talk, mole, pull on me legs," squealed the distressed creature.

Endingen did not hesitate and pulled as hard as he could on the creature's waist and the tops of his legs. With an enormous crash, the soil from above fell through the hole, and Endingen soon felt the weight of the small creature on his back as they both collapsed in a heap on the floor of the tunnel.

They shook the soil off their bodies and stared into each other's startled eyes. The shocked mole said nothing but looked up and down at the mouse that had come crashing into his tunnel and into his life.

"Frankie—Frankie the field mouse—at your service. Now that was an entrance, eh? Eh?" the mouse said excitedly.

Endingen let out a nervous giggle and smiled awkwardly. He started to introduce himself. "Hello, I am…" but before he could finish the sentence, Frankie completed it for him.

"You are Endingen Mole, traveling on an adventure, and you're on the lookout for the moles of Lengnau."

Amazed, Endingen asked how he knew this. "That crazy old toad sent me to help. Geez"—he sighed—"didn't you read what he wrote to you on your map?"

Since Endingen had not read the note, he did not heed Tobias's advice and made his first mistake when he tried to start a conversation with the very brash-sounding mouse. "Well, Frankie, considering your size, I would have thought entering a molehill wouldn't have been a problem. You're so small, I thought you would have easily fit."

A long silence greeted that remark, and suddenly Frankie's friendly face started to grimace. The small mouse thrust his nose against Endingen's, and his deep, dark eyes bulged beneath his hairy, black eyebrows. "Listen, Mole, let's get something straight here!" he bellowed. "I may be lacking in stature, but believe me, around here I am considered a giant. And do you know why?" he continued.

Endingen said nothing, and meekly shook his head.

"'Cause I get things sorted," he screeched. "Around here I am known as 'gets it sorted Frankie.' Whatever you need, I will get it sorted for you, at a price."

Endingen listened again and said nothing. In full agreement, he nodded his head. He was so startled (and a bit frightened), he was not going to inquire what the price to be paid was. Endingen apologized and explained that he had meant nothing by the comment. He was simply very confused by the events that had come crashing down from above.

Frankie smiled a toothy smile and nodded, and in a way, it seemed as though he had accepted Endingen's apology. From that moment on, any mention of size or ability to solve problems was never made again. Endingen was learning quickly exactly what type of person Frankie was, and the fact that someone should never be judged simply by appearance.

"OK, what grub you got" inquired Frankie.

"I am sorry—grub?" Endingen had never heard of the word.

"Food, food…I am starving, and I can't sort things for you on an empty stomach, can I?" Frankie huffed impatiently. Luckily for Endingen, they shared the same appreciation for food and greedy devoured a huge pile of worms.

During the meal, which took more than three hours, Endingen explained his past and the adventures he had experienced on his journey so far, speaking with boundless enthusiasm about Boris and Tobias. Frankie smiled and nodded, smiled and nodded. He was very taken by this friendly, young mole. He sat scratching his whiskery chin while studying the map, and then he stood bolt upright, eyes shimmering. A huge grin appeared to stretch across his whole face, from ear to ear.

"SORTED!" he roared, "I have sorted your problem." Endingen's heart fluttered excitedly and then nearly missed a beat when he heard of the plan. Frankie announced that burrowing underground would take far too long, and that it was too difficult to navigate accurately that way. He further explained that he knew the way to Lengnau, and the whereabouts of Mr. and Mrs. Molesworthy, very well, but only aboveground.

Endingen sighed and told him of his nearly fatal attempts at this type of travel before. Frankie smiled and assured him that this time it would be done by night, under cover of darkness, and not to worry.

"Right, Endingen. We need a strong leaf and your loudest voice."

Endingen was baffled and asked why.

"Why? Why?" Frankie laughed. "We need a helping hand to get this journey sorted, and that will come courtesy of a hedgehog that lives very close to here. He is old, and his hearing isn't too good, so we need to shout for the old man's help. He is a very, very unique character." He chuckled. "The general! We need the general!" Frankie raised his paw, saluting the air with a huge grin.

Endingen was puzzled but dutifully found a strong leaf and handed it to Frankie. The search for the general was about to get under way.

Chapter 10

Operation Final Push, and Meeting the General

"General HHP the third, as he is known, is a tactical genius and a leader of men," explained Frankie. "If you need a plan, the general is the only one you need to talk to."

Endingen knew that if he was to ask whether or not Frankie had formulated some kind of plan, he would get a sharp, glancing stare and the assurance that everything was "sorted." So Endingen decided to keep quiet.

"First of all, we need to call him, and this is the tricky part," Frankie continued. He expertly rolled the leaf that Endingen had retrieved into a cone shape, securing it with freshly plucked whiskers from his cheek. "Plenty to spare of these old things." He giggled. Endingen cringed as he plucked yet more whiskers and secured them to the cone.

"Now, Endingen, please position the loud hailing device out of the molehill, and await further instructions." The two friends worked well together, Frankie obviously taking the lead and Endingen quietly assisting and following the now-regimented instructions. "We both have to shout as loud as we can into the device, and if the general is in the area and he knows we need help, he will come," said Frankie.

Endingen nodded in agreement. "What do we shout?" he asked.

"'General, general, call to arms!' Only the general will understand this—he simply loves code words."

On the count of three, the two friends filled their lungs with as much air as they could and roared out the secret code. Over and over again they hollered until, exhausted and breathless and with their chests pounding, they collapsed arm in arm on the floor of the tunnel.

"Now what?" Endingen panted.

"We wait," Frankie replied.

Of course that didn't mean just sit, wait, and do nothing— that meant they had the opportunity to eat and eat and eat. They gorged their way through a huge pile of assorted worms, insects, and bugs, chatting and laughing about their attempts to call the general.

Frankie was quietly resting when Endingen noticed his large ears twitching. "Did you hear that?" Frankie said to Endingen.

"No, what was it?" Endingen replied quizzically.

"That, my friend, is the sound of an approaching general."

Endingen strained to hear. At first, he heard nothing but the wind whistling down the drafty tunnel, which he quickly dismissed. Then came a sound he couldn't dismiss. A huge, booming voice rumbled down the tunnel, "Corporal Francis, corporal on parade!"

"Corporal Francis?" Endingen inquired. "Who's that?"

"That is what the general calls me, and please don't laugh. We are late for parade. Follow me, and don't say a word," Frankie pleaded.

Frankie and Endingen clambered out of the tunnel and onto the wet grass, where they were immediately greeted by the most magnificent sight. Directly in front of them was a huge, barrel-chested, powerful-looking hedgehog, standing very tall on his hind legs. Sharp gray and black spines adorned his back. Staring straight at Frankie and Endingen was a set of very intense; deep, dark, brown; almost hypnotic eyes.

Frankie stood tall, shuffled to one side, raised a paw, and—with one sharp motion—gave a very snappy salute. At the same time he vigorously shouted, "Corporal Francis Field Mouse and a civilian called Endingen Mole, on parade and ready for your inspection, sir!"

There was a long, silent pause. Endingen stood stiff and motionless as the great hedgehog returned the salute and proceeded to turn in his direction and sniff up and down the young mole's body, from head to tail.

"Good, good," the hedgehog said, nodding and then smiling. "Horatio Hogrunt Pricklesworthy the Third," he said by way of introduction. "You can call me 'sir' or 'general'—it's up to you, although I prefer 'general.'"

Endingen stuttered, "Thank you, sir, ah, I mean general. It is an honor to meet you at last." Endingen couldn't help but stare at the large patches of pink skin on the general's left side that were missing the huge, sharp spines.

The general looked over at Endingen and winked. "Young Endingen Mole, look at me closely. Don't worry, I know what you have been staring at. As you can see, time—and many adventures—are taking their toll. I have had many, many battles, and as you can see," he continued, "I have lost a bit of the old armament along the way, dear boy. I have had many fine victories, and many brave soldiers have stood by my side. However, I have lost many fine men to *him*..." He paused, bowed his head, closed his eyes, and trembled. In a hushed voice, he whispered, "...my greatest foe."

Then, as quickly lightning flashing, his gloomy face changed into one with a soft smile, and he turned toward Frankie. With a huge smile now spreading from cheek to cheek, he spoke with a much softer and affectionate tone. "Now then, Corporal Francis, I understand you and your friend here have gotten yourselves into a bit of a pickle? Splendid! How can I help?"

At this point, both Frankie and Endingen sat next to the general and spent hours recounting the adventures so far. They looked at the map and discussed at length exactly what they considered to be the many challenges facing them.

Endingen's confidence soared when the general asked him for a full mission briefing. Standing to attention, Endingen gave his intelligence report to the general, who eagerly nodded at his every word. "General," Endingen announced, "we can only travel above ground at night. During the day, there are simply too many dangerous creatures watching our every move."

"Dangerous creatures—excellent," replied the general.

"At night it is hard to navigate without moonlight, and the weather is cloudy at the moment," Endingen continued.

"Poor weather, navigation problems—wonderful!" exclaimed the general.

"And the dark wood near the moles' home is...is..." Endingen paused.

"Go on, go on!" boomed the general.

"Well, you know who lives *there*," replied Endingen, his voice full of dread.

"Certain heavy fire from the sky, courtesy of Terrifying Talons—absolutely splendid!" the general exclaimed.

The briefing was complete. The general was very impressed with Endingen's thorough briefing and thought he had the makings of a very good officer one day. With the customary huge smile returning to his face, he stood up, towering over Endingen and Frankie. His huge, barrelled chest expanded, and his powerful, booming voice erupted. "My dear, brave boys, a great hero of mine once said, 'A pessimist sees the difficulty in every opportunity—an optimist sees the opportunity in every difficulty.' Gentlemen, I have a feeling you would do just fine in a scrape, and a scape we will no doubt encounter, but I will be proud to have you stand by me in battle. I therefore hereby declare Operation Final Push is to commence at sunset. HOORAH!" he bellowed.

Endingen and Frankie saluted the general and were dismissed in order to prepare for the impending operation. There was no sign of fear or trepidation, even though in just a few short hours they would be ready for the final push.

Chapter II

Taming Terrifying Talons

S unset was soon upon the three brave soldiers as they set forth on their journey, carefully following the map and the detailed directions they had agreed on. A series of way points marked on the map would allow them to take shelter, rest, and plan each part of their journey. They would also rehearse certain maneuvers just in case, as the general would say, "Things get a little bit interesting."

There were a total of four way points. To reach each one, they estimated, would take two hours, meaning that if they had an incident-free journey, they should be at their destination in time for a well-earned breakfast.

Way point one was close to a large oak tree, where they ate and slept—unfortunately, for only a very short time, as the general was very strict in regard to mission timekeeping. Endingen was put in charge of "stocking up the rations" as the general liked to call it. Food, luckily, was in abundance, and the little mole was happy to busily burrow down in the moist soil to gather tasty snacks.

After they had "fueled up," another popular phrase used by the general, they were briefed on the journey to the next way point. They had developed a series of code words, which required a great deal of coordinated teamwork to make sure they knew exactly what to do and when to do it. Endingen found this extremely exciting.

STANDBY: One of the team had noticed something unusual, and they must all take cover.

SITREP: Short for "situation report." The general would shout this if he required an update as to the situation, or if he needed further orders to move in certain directions.

TALLYHO: A dangerous situation had been identified, and defensive action was needed immediately. As soon as this was shouted, the general would lay on his back. Endingen would lay flat on the left flank of the general's spineless stomach, and Frankie on the right side. The general would then roll into a tight ball and the able lookouts would direct him left, right, forward, and backward.

BRACE, BRACE: Warning of an imminent attack

LAUNCH ARMAMENT: Launch offensive operations, when the situation required them to retaliate.

SPLENDID: The mission had been successful, and they had arrived safely at their destination.

"Right, men," the general boomed, "the next way point is on the edge of the wood. I don't see too many problems getting there, but we must be prepared for possible threats when we arrive."

"Threats?" inquired Endingen. "Could you explain please, General?"

"Certainly...will do, young man," the general replied. "Terrifying Talons is a very old tawny owl who sits in a huge oak tree on the edge of the wood, watching and waiting for his prey. He is a great hunter, and he and I have had many, many encounters over the years. Every time I have passed close to the wood, he has attacked me. Luckily, I have always managed to escape the full grip of his legendry talons. But he has taken some trophies with him." The general chuckled while pointing to the area of missing spines on his side. "I really fear that the next time we meet I might not be so lucky."

Endingen gulped and felt his heart race.

"To make sure we will stand a chance in a confrontation, we must remember to carry out all of the drills I have taught you. Fear not, men," the general said with confidence, "this time we shall be ready for him, and we will have a real surprise in store."

The wind was now increasing in strength, leaves rustling along the edge of the wood. The sounds of the usually noisy night creatures had disappeared. It seemed they were hiding from something or someone. The rain continued to lash down into their eyes, and the dark night seemed to be getting eerily darker.

A large area of deep, lush grass marked their arrival at way point two. So far, the journey had been totally incident free. But as they sat down to have some supper, Endingen, although he did not look outwardly worried, was beginning to feel very tense indeed.

"OK, gentlemen," the general whispered, "here is where things may get interesting. We are presently here, and the residence of Mr. and Mrs. Albert Molesworthy is just over here." The general continued with his long briefing. This was the most critical and dangerous phase of the entire operation. "A very slow and stealthy approach will be the order of the day," he reminded Frankie and Endingen. "We must make sure we don't stand out or look suspicious in any way."

After a short break, they were ready to go. Endingen's excitement level was at an all-time high. He simply couldn't wait to finally meet the Lengnau moles.

Frankie and the general both had very serious expressions. It was as though they knew that soon something serious might happen. Neither of them spoke of their fear as they set out very slowly, staying close to the ground and as near to cover as they could. It seemed that they had been traveling much longer than Endingen had imagined they would. His feet were aching and the rucksack on his back felt uncomfortable and very heavy.

"Not long now, men," the general whispered as they started to pass along the edge of the forest.

Endingen smiled at Frankie, but the mouse only managed a half smile in return. He was looking very anxious. The smile soon turned to a frown as he shouted, "STANDBY!" as loudly as he could.

"What is it? What is it? SITREP!" the general demanded.

Frankie's reply was short, sharp, and very to the point. "Oak tree, nine o'clock, bright sparks seen! TALLYHO!"

Immediately, the general lay flat on his back shouting, "Defensive positions, men! Go, go, go!"

With great precision, Endingen and Frankie leaped into their positions.

"STANDBY!" shouted the general, as his huge muscular body rose high, bent over, and rolled into a well-defended, spiny sphere. This well-rehearsed defensive maneuver was complete before Endingen could take a breath. "Right, lads, now we wait and see what we are dealing with here. Only on your orders will we move."

"Understood, General!" the lookouts shouted back.

"SITREP, Endingen!" the general ordered.

Endingen peered out and gazed at the tree in the distance. The large, black silhouette of the fir tree contained a winged figure. Below the figure, he could clearly see a series of large, bright, white and amber sparks flying into the air, and at the same time he heard a very loud scraping sound. He duly reported this to the general; it was met a long pause.

"OK, gentlemen, what you have heard and seen is Talons getting ready to attack. He is making sure his weapons are sharp."

"Corporal Francis, when he is within ten yards of us, give the order."

"Yes sir, ten yards, sir," Frankie replied.

The general moved sideways in the direction of the tree. It seemed as though he wanted to provoke a reaction from the owl.

In his position, Endingen was facing away and could not see what was happening. The wind seem to stop. The muffled heartbeat of the general and the constant SITREPS from Frankie were part of the mixture of muffled noises Endingen heard. He was feeling very frightened. The scraping sounds soon gave way to the sound of beating wings.

"He is getting ready," squealed Frankie.

Whoosh, whoosh. The beating was getting faster and faster, and at this point, so was Endingen's heartbeat.

"BRACE, BRACE!" shouted the general.

Endingen closed his eyes tightly and held his breath as he heard a series of eerie screeches and beating wings. Talons had seen them and was diving in to attack.

Frankie screamed deafeningly, "LAUNCH ARMAMENT!" The general's body squeezed downward very quickly and exerted a massive amount of pressure on Endingen and Frankie. Any breath that they had was squashed from their lungs.

The deafening sound of the general's spines flying into the air was quickly followed by a series of great thudding noises. Screeches and squeals were followed by a feverish, uncontrollable flapping sound, then…silence.

"SITREP, Corporal Francis!" boomed the general.

"Multiple direct hits, sir. Enemy sent packing, sir."

"BRAVO!" shouted the general as his body uncoiled.

Endingen gasped and choked and then looked at Frankie and the general. All three grinned, punched the air in triumph, and chorused, "BRAVO!" Terrifying Talons, the tawny owl, had been well and truly tamed.

There was no time to celebrate, so the victorious team scuttled off toward a small outcrop of corn. This was way point three. Here they rested and spoke at length about their battle with the owl. The general basked in the glory of what he called his greatest victory.

"Right, gentlemen, at the end of that last set of cornstalks should be the entrance to the residence of Mr. and Mrs. Molesworthy," the general said confidently. "Keep your eyes peeled and ears pricked. We are looking for a small metal covering and the sound of running water and, if we are lucky, singing."

They inched their way along the cornfield and then stopped abruptly when Frankie sounded the code word that Endingen had yearned for. "SPLENDID!" Frankie yelled as he pointed to a small metal plate overgrown with grass. Soon they were greeted by the sound of gurgling water.

They all looked at each other and silently embraced, holding each other tightly. Tears of both sadness and happiness fell from their eyes.

The general and Frankie stepped back, looked straight at Endingen, and saluted him. "Young Endingen Mole, it has been our pleasure to stand by you during our greatest conflict," the general stated. "You have showed great courage and strength in the face of danger. Now marks the next chapter in your adventure. I am sure it will be full of excitement and great pleasure. We hope you find everything you are seeking. Be assured that we will always be close by, should you ever need us. Farewell, and may our paths cross again one day.

"Corporal Francis—dismissed!" ordered the general.

"Yes, sir, with pleasure, sir," Frankie replied with a huge smile.

Endingen watched with great sadness as his two friends turned, waved, and hurried off toward the cornfield just as the sun began to peek over the nearby hills. He took a moment to reflect and contentedly sighed, and then he dug down toward the sound of the running water.

Chapter 12

The Truth Revealed

Endingen's nose broke the last pieces of soil; at last he was in a tunnel. It was not the type of small, drafty, musty-smelling tunnel he was used to. This one smelled of perfume and was extremely neat and tidy. His nose started to twitch excitedly as a delicious smell greeted the very hungry young mole. It was such a delicious smell that his stomach let out a huge gurgling sound as he made his way along the tunnel.

In the distance, he could just make out a very large, wooden door, and when he peered closer, he saw a welcome plaque hanging off a very large, brass door handle in the center of the door. The plaque read:

Welcome to the residence of Albert and Edwina Molesworthy
Please knock loudly

Before he knocked, Endingen put his ear close to the door and listened. He heard the sound of running water and a soft, womanly voice singing a very happy-sounding melody. Endingen smiled, and with all of his strength, he banged out three huge, loud knocks on the large, wooden door. He listened again and heard a man's voice this time.

"Can you get the door, Mother? I have just plunged my old, aching bones into the bath."

"Oh dear, Father, that's just typical of you…just as I have nearly finished all of my baking," another voice said with a sigh.

Endingen stepped away slightly as the door opened slowly. The lady mole looked at Endingen with a very intrigued expression, and he stared back similarly.

"Father," she shouted suddenly, "Father! Come quick. It's him! He's here!" Her short paws reached out and pulled Endingen into a huge, furry embrace. Tears rolled down her cheeks. "My darling, my darling, you're here."

Endingen looked very confused and said in a bewildered voice, "I think you may be confused, madam. We have never met before."

The gentleman mole, wrapped from head to foot in a large bathing gown, was now standing by the lady's side. They both smiled and with one voice said, "But we know who you are. The map you hold will provide us all with many answers to many questions."

Endingen by this stage was completely baffled. He shook his head and wondered what he would say or do next.

"Mother, offer our guest some refreshments, please."

"Of course, Father, how rude of me! And I am sorry, please call us Albert and Edwina,"

she said politely.

Endingen followed Albert into the kitchen area, a part of the residence that obviously saw a lot of activity. A large table was adorned with many seats, and the table was piled high with all kinds of elaborate mole food: worm puddings, bug casseroles, and—Endingen's particular favourite—rotten-seasonal-fruit pie.

The kitchen sink was piled high with cooking pots and baking tins waiting to be washed and put neatly away. Albert and Edwina had obviously been expecting guests to call.

Endingen's stomach let out another embarrassingly loud groan. "Well, well," Albert said with a chuckle, "someone around here is a bit peckish. Sit yourself in front of the fire and get warm, young man."

Edwina joined Albert, and they offered Endingen many delicious home-cooked foods, which of course he devoured gratefully. He spent what seemed hours recalling all of his adventures. Albert and Edwina quizzed him about his earliest memories of his life before he decided to embark on his travels and about the reasons behind his decision to undertake such a dangerous journey.

As Endingen sat back to relax, after eating probably half his own weight in food, he looked up and was met by Albert and Edwina staring at him very intently. "Oh, oh," he said, "my apologies. Would you like to see the map?" He handed the map to Albert, who in turn handed it to Edwina.

She stared at it for what seemed to be a very long time and then shook her head while whispering something into Albert's ear. He stared long and hard at the map and started to shake his head. Suddenly, he shouted out, "Bless my old bones, I have got it, Mother! Be a dear and pass me a candle, please."

Edwina passed him the candle, and he started to wave it across the bottom right edge of the map, over and over again. "Well I never!" he exclaimed triumphantly. "Come, both of you, and look."

At the bottom of the map, now very clear, appeared some very beautiful handwriting that Endingen had never seen before. It read:

> *If you are reading this map, we must let you know of its purpose. This map is the property of the Tobler family and shows the location of our most valued and trusted friends. In the event of anything happening to us during these very uncertain times, the bearer of this map must travel to the persons mentioned herewith and seek guidance and direction to the Tobler grand residence, Hillfoot House. This residence has been in the Tobler family for many, many years and shall be handed down to future generations of the Tobler family. Be of good heart and faith, take up the Tobler name and family values, and make Hillfoot House your home.*
>
> *Stephen and Winifred Tobler*

Endingen was speechless. He was also a little confused and shocked, and looked toward Edwina and Albert for an explanation. They recognized that the young mole needed some answers. Putting their paws around his shoulders, they led him through to the lounge room. He sat down with a hot cup of tea in a very comfortable, grand leather chair. Albert leaned across to him and with a very soothing voice began his tale.

"My dear, dear young mole, I will not hide the truth from you. That message was from your father and mother, who were sadly taken from us in a tragic accident shortly after your birth. Great storms had broken riverbanks, and all of the nearby lands were flooded. Sadly, the storm waters washed away your parents' home. We never received any news about what happened to you all. Regretfully, we assumed that you all had suffered the same terrible fate."

Albert and Edwina bowed their heads and moaned mournfully, quietly shedding a few tears before looking up at Endingen, now smiling huge and friendly smiles. "Welcome to your uncle and auntie's humble home, our wonderful nephew, Master Thomas Tobler. It seems that all along you were meant to go on your journey and find us, and you didn't even know."

Thomas smiled meekly and asked if it was OK to take some rest, as it had been a day that he would never forget.

"Of course, my darling, let us show you to your room."

Chapter 13

Master Thomas Tobler

"Thomas Tobler…Endingen Mole…my parents washed away in a storm…Hillfoot House…family values…Oh dear, oh dear." He sobbed. "What is to become of me?" Confusion, insecurity, and exhaustion had taken their toll on the little mole. Eventually, as he drifted off to sleep, he wondered if anything would be clearer to him in the morning.

"Lovely cup of tea, dearest Thomas?" a soft voice whispered to him. "You have been sleeping for two whole days. How are you feeling?"

Thomas smiled when he started to recognize that the soft voice belonged to Aunty Edwina, and his heart raced as her warm and sweet-smelling paws embraced him. He now knew that as long as he was with his aunty and uncle, things would start to become clearer. He also had a very strong feeling that this was only the start of his adventures, and that he would have to travel many more paths in order to find out who Thomas Tobler really was.

Days had now passed, and although Thomas had been made to feel very comfortable and extremely welcome in his aunt and uncle's home, deep down inside he wanted to know more about Hillfoot House and exactly how he was to travel there to take up his inheritance. But above all, he knew he must live up to the family values that his late parents had spoken of. The subject simply couldn't wait anymore. Soon Thomas and his aunt and uncle sat down to talk more about the inheritance and the story of Hillfoot House.

First, Uncle Albert, who had his head bowed low, spoke in a very hushed tone. "I was hoping that this subject would not come up, and that you would be happy to stay here with Mother and me."

Aunty Edwina nodded in agreement and continued, "You must understand that we are very concerned for your safety, Thomas. It has taken you so long to be a part of our lives, and now it seems you want to leave us to chase a dream."

Thomas shook his head and replied, "This isn't a dream—this was the wish of my parents, and so I must go to Hillfoot House and claim it for my own." Thomas could see that they were getting upset at the thought of him leaving so soon after arriving, but he was determined that this was what he was destined to do and that nothing would stop him. "Aunty and uncle," he said cheerfully, "I am very grateful for all that you have done for me and your concerns for my safety, but as I have told you, I have been on a great journey already with many dangers and got here safely and in one piece."

Both his aunty and uncle nodded slowly and sighed. "Sadly, we knew that you would want to continue on to Hillfoot House, and we understand, but we are concerned and worried," Uncle Albert said. "The journey will be difficult, and when you get there, we both know who is already there, and the danger you could face from…" He paused, and then he and Aunt Edwina said together with a single, trembling voice, "*Him.*"

Thomas was now puzzled. "Who, exactly, is this 'him' that you are referring to?" he asked.

Once again his aunty and uncle, with heads bowed, let out a sigh. "He is your Uncle Julius, the brother of your late mother and me," Uncle Albert explained, "and someone that we do not like to speak about. But as you have made up your mind to go, you must know about him. He is someone you will have to face if you want to claim what is rightfully yours, Thomas."

Aunty Edwina now took her turn and explained in detail the story of Uncle Julius. "Julius was always very jealous of both your uncle and your mother because we found happiness when we were married. Julius has never been married, and has always had only one interest—himself. When your father built Hillfoot House for his family, Julius was very jealous and claimed that, as a family member, he was entitled to reside there. Bitter arguments raged until, in the end, your father and mother and both of us told Julius that Hillfoot House was only for our children as a legacy, and that he would not be allowed to reside there.

"Julius became very bitter and vowed that one day Hillfoot House would be his and his alone. He moved away, and for years he had not been seen nor heard from, until the tragic storm took your parents. We were all still mourning their passing when news reached us that your Uncle Julius had moved into Hillfoot House, and he has been there ever since. He has become very wealthy using Hillfoot House as a residence for some very untrustworthy and fearsome folk."

Uncle Albert placed a reassuring paw around Thomas's shoulders and sighed. "If you try and claim Hillfoot House as your inheritance, you will be placing yourself in real danger, Thomas. Please get a good night's sleep and think about this carefully."

That night, Thomas thought about all that his uncle and aunty had said, and he stared at the map until the wee hours. Although it would be easy to stay forever with his new family, whom he cared for deeply, he needed adventure in his life and, most of all, he needed to follow the wishes of his parents by taking the Tobler name, following the family values, and making Hillfoot House a home for him and his future family.

In the morning he would have to break the news to his aunt and uncle that he had made up his mind to leave. Although he knew that they would be upset by his decision, he hoped that they would understand. Thomas snuggled down into his warm bed and slowly drifted off to sleep, listening to the soft singing voice of his aunty as she took her late night bath. He sighed contentedly and felt very secure and warm. Aunty Edwina was singing a beautiful lullaby about him.

Thomas has come, and now Thomas will go.
Is this wise? Only time will tell; I just don't know.
Too short, but very sweet our reunion has been;
coming back to us safely is our heartfelt dream.
A long and dangerous journey he will make,
to where Hillfoot House lays with Julius in wait.
He needs someone to guide him, watch over him, and help him learn,
as danger surely awaits at every turn.
Henrietta, Sebastian, and our friends in the trees I must call
so Thomas will return one day, safe and sound, to his loved ones, friends, and all.

Chapter 14

The Journey to Hillfoot House Begins

Thomas awoke after a very long and deep sleep. He was feeling excited. Today was the day that he was to embark on another journey. This time his goal was to search for Hillfoot House and find his Uncle Julius so that he could claim his inheritance. He looked around his room for his rucksack—he couldn't wait to start packing.

At the same time, his mind was reflecting back on the words his Aunty Edwina had mentioned while singing her lullaby, in particular the names she had sung about.

He sat on the end of the bed and started to study his map. He soon recognized all of the names in her lullaby. He carefully marked their locations with a pencil, knowing that he would need help from all of them if he stood any chance of successfully finding his way to Hillfoot House.

"First things first, though," he thought. He had to break the news that today he was going to leave his aunty and uncle for a while and go, once again, out into the unknown.

To his surprise, as he made his way to the kitchen, both his aunty and uncle greeted him with huge smiles and warm embraces. "Ready for your trip, Thomas?" they chorused.

"Well…yes, but how did you know?" he stuttered.

"Our dear Thomas," his uncle said as he knelt down and looked straight into Thomas's eyes. "From the first day we met and you told us of your adventures, we knew the kind of mole you are, and that you take after your mother and father in that respect."

Thomas looked quizzically at him and shook his head. "The sense of adventure," his uncle said, chuckling. "Your parents had it before you, and now you have it. The Tobler family all seem to want to live their lives seeking adventures and getting into scrapes, but at the same time meeting lots of interesting folk along the way who end up sharing in your adventures. I am afraid it is obvious to us that our very unadventurous life is not for you, my lad," Uncle Albert continued, smiling widely. "So, we want to help you as much as we can to make sure you are very well prepared for you adventures." He pointed at the kitchen table.

Thomas stood on the tip of his paws and gasped as he saw what seemed to be a small mountain of food. All of his avourite home-cooked foods were on display and being packed into separate wooden containers, all neatly marked. His nose twitched excitedly at all of the delicious smells.

He looked over at some smaller containers. They were marked "Especially for," words that were followed by the names of many types of animals. Aunty Edwina smiled and remarked, "Well, you have to be prepared—you never know who you might bump into along the way."

One box in particular caught his eye. It was smaller than the others and was fastened tightly with an old, red wax seal and marked "For Julius Only." Thomas was intrigued. "What does Uncle Julius like to eat?" he remarked.

His aunty seemed flustered. "Oh…oh…that's a little something special for your uncle, a gift from both of us," she stuttered.

"Can I look?" Thomas said innocently.

"No, no, absolutely not, it is a surprise, and he simply loves surprises. Now run along and bring us your rucksack," she replied, guiding Thomas back toward his bedroom.

He collected his rucksack. When he came back to the table, he saw that this time all of the containers had been wrapped very securely in a dark gray material bound by pieces of string.

"Why is everything wrapped up like that?" he inquired.

"Because of the storms, Thomas," his uncle replied. "All of the wise folk around here have been talking, and they are warning that great storms are coming very soon."

"You need to protect yourself on your journey from the wild weather that is coming," his aunty continued. "Staying dry and warm at all times is vitally important, so we have wrapped all of your food and other essential items that you will need in water-proof cloth."

Just as he was about to ask exactly what the essential items were, Uncle Albert started to read off a checklist. "How very mole-like and strangely familiar," Thomas thought as he chuckled to himself.

Enough delicious food for our wonderful nephew and other adventurous types. *Check.*

Portable headlamp. *Check.*

Trusty compass. *Check.*

Individual tent for aboveground shelter. Check.

Personal cleaning and grooming kit—very important to make a good first impression. *Check.*

Our home clearly marked on the map, so you can find you way back again. *Double check.*

Candleholder, candles, and rain cover. *Check.*

Special gift for *him. Check.*

At this point his uncle and aunty stopped, sank to their knees, and held Thomas tightly in their paws. They whispered, "Thomas, please promise us you will come back safe. Your journey will be long, the weather treacherous, and the outcome uncertain. Make sure you listen to all of the advice that our friends will give you, and follow your heart. Come back to us soon, our dearest Thomas."

Thomas began to feel slightly nervous now as he listened closely to their words, but he knew that the journey he was about to make was what he was destined to do. "Of course I will listen to them, Aunty, and I will take care of myself, Uncle. I promise you both that I will always follow my heart, and one day I will find my way back to you."

Their embrace got tighter and tighter as his aunty and uncle listened to him speak. Thomas knew that he had found family that made him feel safe and happy, and who would always look after him.

He was determined to keep his promises as he placed the now very heavy rucksack on his back and made his way slowly toward the front door. He lit one of the candles and placed the rain cover over it, and then he smiled and looked back at his Aunty Edwina and Uncle Albert. They stood closely together, wiping away tears from their eyes and trying to smile bravely. Taking a deep breath, Thomas said nothing. He just smiled, blew a kiss, and waved slowly as he closed the door behind himself.

As he made his way down the drafty tunnel, he heard the echoes of his aunty sobbing and the voice of his uncle trying to console her. "There, there, Mother, we always hoped that one day he would come into our lives, and now we pray he will return again one day. He is a Tobler. Let's pray that he chooses the right path and makes the right decisions."

Thomas shivered as the wind rushed into the tunnel. The air was damp and bitterly cold. "No turning back now," he said to himself. He tightened the straps on his rucksack and dug with all of his strength toward a small pinprick of light that marked the exit hole into the world outside.

Chapter 15

Listening and Learning Lessons

When his head pierced through the soil, it was met with the most tremendous cold and wet wind. By the time Thomas managed to burrow completely out, the force of the wind had blown out his candle, and he was starting to feel his fur getting very wet and cold. Leaves and grass were blowing in every direction. He had never experienced such powerful gusts of wind; they nearly blew him off his paws. He needed to find shelter, and to find it quickly.

There was just enough moonlight for him to see his map; he couldn't light his candle, and his headlamp was packed deep in his rucksack, which by now was completely wet and seemed to weigh twice as much as it had when he was in the tunnel.

He moved slowly forward, crouched over under the weight of his rucksack. He started to breathe heavily as he made his way toward the edge of a forest, where he could set up some sort of shelter for the night. There were no sounds, no familiar calls from other animals, just the incredible blasts of cold air constantly blowing him from side to side.

Tears ran down his face as the freezing wind blew directly into his eyes. The grass and mud beneath him was soaking his paws. He started to shiver and shake, and his teeth started to chatter uncontrollably. He was so very cold, and very alone...

To keep his spirits up, he thought of being with the general, and especially how he had felt in the heat of their battle with Terrifying Talons. He remembered the general telling him that he was brave and courageous and that when times were hard, his bravery and courage would shine through.

It was true, as by now he had started to move more freely and wasn't thinking of or feeling the cold anymore; he felt only a warm glow inside from his memories of exciting times spent with his friends. He wiped away the muddy and damp deposits on his glasses, and, straining his eyes, he could see the outline of trees in the distance.

As he neared the wood, he noticed that all of the tree branches were smashing against the trunks, making loud booming and crashing noises. He spotted a large ash tree that had a deep, sunken area in between two very large roots. Thomas breathed a sigh of relief and, hurrying as fast as his cold little paws could carry him, made his way toward the ash tree.

Crack, crack!

Thomas looked up. A large branch from the ash tree came crashing down toward him. He threw himself forward to try and get out of the way of the branch, but he was so burdened down with his heavy rucksack that he simply couldn't move fast enough.

He felt the weight of the branch hit his rucksack with another huge crack, and then he heard the rustle of hundreds of leaves as smaller branches hit him on his back and arms. Then silence.

Thomas felt a huge weight on his back. As he strained his neck to look over his shoulder, he could just make out that the branch was pinning him to the ground. He soon began to feel an intense ache coming from his left leg. He couldn't move the leg much before the pain took his breath away. Thomas knew he was injured but he also that he had to get free of the branch and make it to the large ash tree.

His rucksack had been thrown off his back and was lying a short distance away. Thomas reached out as far as he could manage, but he couldn't quite touch his rucksack.

"Be brave, be courageous!" he shouted at the top of his voice, and with one huge push, he managed to grab his rucksack. He was now breathing harder and harder, trying to muster up enough strength to keep pushing and pushing and pushing.

He held his rucksack with one paw and dug down with the other to try to grip some small tree roots and set himself free. Then, with a last deep breath and push, the pressure from the tree branch was gone. Thomas had managed to wriggle free, and he now limped to the safety of the large tree.

Breathing hard and shaking, he felt the pain in his leg getting worse. He collapsed in a heap. He managed to open up his tent, and in a few moments, he was out of the wind and rain. For the first time in what seemed hours, he began to feel warm. He felt even warmer as he opened up the delicious boxes of foods that his aunty had packed for him, and although the pain in his leg was still a concern, he was so exhausted that he soon drifted into a deep sleep.

When he woke up, it was still dark, the wind was still howling outside his tent, and the pain he was feeling now was more intense. He remembered all the stories the general had told of getting into scrapes and patching himself up when he was hurt.

Thomas smiled and set about finding three large sticks, two of which he would use to make a splint to support his leg and the other of which he would use as a walking stick. These were easy to find, as many branches had fallen from the mighty ash tree, and soon Thomas had his leg well supported and had a sturdy walking stick in his paw. He was ready to continue his journey.

Once again he smiled as he thought of the wise words of the general. "Planning, my dear boy, planning and preparation are essential if one is to be successful." With this thought in mind, Thomas put on the portable headlamp, checked his map with the compass, and carefully marked his route. He would go around the edge of the wood, turn left turn at a large cornfield, and then follow the field straight ahead toward the river.

Thomas packed his tent and the rest of his belongings into his rucksack and then started to hobble very slowly toward the edge of the forest. The wind seemed to have dropped and the rain had eased, and now he could hear the chatter of all of the woodland creatures as the sun's first light was noticeable.

Although his progress was now very slow and he was in great discomfort, Thomas kept thinking of his adventures and of all of the folk he had met along the way. He smiled contentedly. He heard a distant whispering sound and, as he looked up, saw the tops of tall cornstalks waving in the breeze. He stopped and checked his map and compass again; he was near the cornfield. "Not far now," he thought.

The very tall corn was turning from a green to a brown color as the delicious, sweet corn began to ripen. All Thomas was interested in, though, was finding cover, as in the distance, he could hear the calls of many birds of prey eager to start their hunt as the sun was rising. Thomas stooped and checked his map and compass once more, his ears twitching as he heard the sound of fast-moving water. He was close, very close, to the river.

He decided that he would have to make the quickest dash that he could from the cornfield to the river, and he again thought of what the general might advise. "Camouflage, my dear chap, camouflage! Cover your body up, and the enemy won't recognize you."

Thomas threw the rucksack over his back and placed corn leaves and stalks all over both himself and his heavy rucksack. He threw away the splint protecting his leg and started to crawl toward the riverbank.

Slowly, inch by inch, he crawled, stopping occasionally to hear the sound of the gushing water but also to check that he wasn't being seen from above. No screeching of birds above meant that, by moving very slowly, he wasn't being noticed. It was clear to Thomas that he had learned many important things from his friends, in particular the general.

The grass now disappeared and was replaced by stones. The noise from the river became incredibly loud. His camouflage had worked so well, he was safe in between a group of spindly trees next to the fast-moving and very high river. Thomas opened up his rucksack and enjoyed a short breakfast as he watched the sun rise slowly over the cornfield. He smiled and muttered to himself, "The general was right again—preparation and planning are key."

He then became distracted and looked all around as he could hear someone singing a song over and over again.

> *Hoi, hoi, Sali and hoi*
> *Get off my river, you naughty boy*
> *One fish, two fish, three, and four—if I am lucky a good few more*
> *Seize the day, seize the day, ha, ha, this is Sebastian's law*
> *Hoi, hoi, Sali and hoi*
> *Henrietta my ladyship, prim, proper, but oh so coy*
> *Her ladyship will snap, her ladyship will scream*
> *Getting rid of this strange old shrew is her life's dream*
> *Her ladyship, Sebastian and Thomas will soon be together*
> *In a place of sadness, pain, sorrow that will be felt forever*
> *But brightness is at hand for it is carved in silver shining bright across this land.*
> *Hoi, hoi, Sali and hoi*
> *Sebastian Shrew, old, gray, strange but jolly and always full of joy.*

Chapter 16

Long Legs and Fishing Poles

As Thomas crept closer and closer to the river's edge, he could make out all of the words being sung. The song started off very jolly and funny, which made him chuckle; then he heard worrying words such as "pain" and "sorrow."

Thomas had to investigate further. He knew that this could mean only one thing: Sebastian the strange shrew must be very close by. He climbed slowly up the highest ridge overlooking the river. In the distance, among the nettle and bramble bushes, he saw a clearing that ran down to the edge of the river. He made his way down very slowly, listening to the song and wondering where Sebastian might be. He spent a while looking all around, until he spotted something very unfamiliar.

It was a small sailing boat that was tied up to an old tree trunk. The twisted trunk was covered in deep-green moss. The boat had obviously seen better times; it looked as though it had been used daily for a long time without the owner taking good care of it. All of its wooden planks were splintered, and the paint had fallen away, and where there once would have been a flag, there were now just a few shreds of cloth.

On the front of the boat was a plaque. It read…"Oh no," thought Thomas, "I cannot pronounce it. Carp Deem…no, no, that's not right. Carpet Diam…no, no, not right either." Thomas was ready for one last try at pronouncing the name when he was interrupted by a croaky, little voice coming from the far riverbank.

"It is pronounced '*carpe diem*,' my boy, and, if you are an educated fellow like myself, you will know that it means 'seize the day.' That is exactly what we need to do! Now, come closer where I can have a good look at you." Thomas left his rucksack and, supported by his homemade walking stick, hobbled slowly toward the small figure ahead.

The shrew was small, about half the size of Thomas. His face was very hairy with huge whiskers. He had deep and clear brown eyes. He wore what looked to be waterproof clothes, similar to those Thomas was wearing. In his hand was a long fishing pole. He was moving it up and down and then twirling it around over and over above his head. Around his neck he wore a brightly colored bow tie. He smiled as he began to sing the song again. Thomas noticed that when he was singing, he was doing so with a huge, toothy smile.

"Stop," the shrew said abruptly. "I am Sebastian. And who might you be?"

"I am Thomas Tobler, and I am seeking a guide to show me the way to Hillfoot House. I have spoken to my family, and they said that maybe you could help." There was a long pause, and all Thomas could hear was the crashing of the fast-moving water against the riverbank.

"Wait!" said the shrew as he jumped straight into the river; he then disappeared. A few minutes passed, and there was no sign of the little shrew. Thomas looked up and down the riverbank, once, twice, and a third time—still no sign of the shrew.

He then felt a soft tap on his back and looked down. He was greeted by two huge front teeth and many more sparkling white teeth; Sebastian's face seemed to be one great big smile.

"Oi, down here," Sebastian continued. "Pleased to meet you, young Thomas. I have heard all about you. You are the talk of so many folk around here. Now, let's get cracking. We have to be somewhere very important very soon, so we need to seize the day and set sail!"

Sebastian guided Thomas to his boat. Thomas was finding it very difficult to walk without tripping over the rocks at the edge of the river. "Righty-ho, here we are! Now hop in." Sebastian chuckled.

Thomas looked at him and grimaced. Couldn't Sebastian see that he was injured and was walking with a stick?

"Come on, boy, jump in my boat," Sebastian said, roaring with laughter.

Thomas was not very impressed.

"It's all right, my lad, just an old shrew's way of having a little fun! Here, let me help you!" Sebastian may have been small, but he threw Thomas's rucksack into the boat with little effort, and soon Thomas was being lifted over the side and into the boat. "Fit as a fiddle, me," Sebastian exclaimed. "I get lots of good exercise running away from her ladyship when she spots me fishing." He chuckled.

His smile now turned to a serious expression, and he spoke with a voice full of authority. "Rules, rules, my boy, I have rules. Number one: when we are travelling in my good vessel, *Carpe Diem*, you, young fellow, will address me as 'skipper,' not 'Sebastian' or 'shrew' or anything else. Just 'skipper'—understand?"

"Not 'captain' or 'admiral'?" Thomas inquired with a smile.

The skipper did not look very amused by his quick and witty reply.

"Yes, Skipper," Thomas replied with a salute.

"Hmmm," came the reply. "The second rule," barked the skipper, "is that you are to obey everything I say while sailing. This river is fast and is flooding the land so our safety is key—understand?"

"Absolutely, Skipper, will comply," Thomas responded, this time more respectfully.

"Cast away, my boy," shouted the skipper as he pushed to launch the boat into the murky and muddy river with a large oar. The good vessel *Carpe Diem*, with the skipper at the helm and Thomas as deckhand, was on its way down the river. Thomas had no idea why, or where they were going. He had never been anywhere near a river, let alone in a boat, and he was being thrown from side to side as the skipper moved the rudder from left to right.

"Rocks, dear boy, lots of nasty rocks on this stretch of the river. If we hit one, we are sunk," explained the skipper.

Just looking at the concentration on the face of the old shrew, Thomas could see that he had been doing this for many years, and that filled him with confidence.

"The rapids are up ahead—time to hold tight!" shouted the skipper loudly over the noise of the pounding water hitting the side of the boat.

Thomas took his advice and held tightly to the ropes hanging from the main mast pole. The boat was thrown very violently up, and then it came crashing down. As this started to happen, the skipper laughed loudly and shouted, "Is that all you have got for us? Come on higher and faster!"

Thomas didn't see the fun at all, and as the boat was being thrown around in the fast white water, he started to feel very ill. Just as he thought the water could not get any more violent, a huge wave of bright white, icy water hit the boat.

Thomas and his rucksack weighed far more than the skipper, and Thomas's side of the boat started to tip over. Soon the fast-moving river started to flood the boat. In what seemed like one movement, the skipper threw the rudder over in the opposite direction at the same time he pulled Thomas and his belongings toward the center of the boat.

"Yes. Yes!" the skipper screamed with delight. "Nice try, but you will never beat the old skipper. Here," he barked, throwing an old bucket toward Thomas, "get bailing."

Thomas was only too happy to. As the boat returned to its normal upright sailing position, he hurriedly bailed out the freezing cold river water from the boat. After a while, Thomas noticed that the skipper was happily humming the tune he had been singing for hours. The river now was calmer, and the water was looking a familiar deep brown color.

"OK, lad, we are nearly there. Get your stuff gathered and ready with the mooring rope, if you please," the skipper said, pointing to a large, coiled rope near the rear of the boat.

Thomas saluted and grabbed the rope as the skipper expertly guided *Carpe Diem* gently onto a muddy embankment at the lowest part of the river.

Before Thomas could do or say anything, the skipper had tied the rope to a large tree trunk with some beautiful knots. He then bowed and looked at Thomas. "My dear fellow, you were a sound shipmate and are welcome to sail with me anytime, but for now, we have somewhere to go and someone very special to see," Sebastian announced as he helped Thomas and his luggage down from the boat. "We haven't much time—we'll have to move silently but quickly."

Thomas again hobbled slowly; his leg was still hurting despite being wrapped tightly in what Sebastian described as "local leaf medicine." They continued slowly with a large crop of corn at their backs and the grassy edge of the river in front of them. The sun by now was high in the sky and casting shadows down onto the path they were following.

"Here is where they are sleeping, forever at peace," Sebastian whispered with a bowed head.

"Who? Where who are sleeping?" Thomas inquired.

Sebastian held tightly onto Thomas's paw and pointed in the direction of a mound of stones close by the riverbank. Thomas stood still and looked ahead. There were flowers everywhere near the rocky shape, all the colors of the rainbow—simply beautiful. In the distance he heard bells chiming. The air was fragrant. This was a place of peace and tranquility.

A long silence was broken when Sebastian dropped to his knees and held onto Thomas tightly with his small paws. "My dearest Thomas, this where I found them after one of the most frightening and violent storms that I have known in my long lifetime. This is where I found your parents."

Thomas said nothing. He just stared at the mound of stones and the beautiful flowers that surrounded them.

Sebastian continued, "I did the right thing and laid them to rest here in a place that is so colorful and peaceful."

Thomas sank to his knees and embraced the old shrew. "Thank you, Sebastian, this is where I needed to be, and you did the right thing. They are at rest, and I shall never forget them," Thomas said in a very hushed voice. He moved away from Sebastian and knelt next to the mound of large stones. Sebastian moved away, into the cornfield.

After a while Thomas moved back toward the cornfield, where he once again embraced Sebastian. This time no words were exchanged, but their individual feelings were kas they looked at each other and smiled. As they looked back toward the river, at the beautiful flowers and the resting place of Thomas's parents, a shadow began to turn everything dark. A huge whoosh and a deep, beating noise seemed to echo from all around. Suddenly, the air was filled with grass and dust.

Thomas and Sebastian both looked toward the sun and the cornfield. The shadow was getting darker and the noise stronger. Sebastian pulled Thomas toward him, looking straight into his eyes. "Her ladyship," he gasped.

Looking down at the grass, Thomas saw well-manicured talons. He looked up, and his gaze was met by a pair of incredibly long legs that seemed to go on forever. As his neck strained so he could look up even farther, he could see beautiful, sparklingly clean white, gray, and black feathers. Finally, standing on the tips of his paws, Thomas saw a long, yellow and black beak. At its end, staring straight at him, were two sparkling, bright orange eyes.

Sebastian bowed several times. Thomas was intrigued. The elegant bird looked at Thomas and then at Sebastian and then back to Thomas. "So," she began, "this is the young mole that everyone is talking about. How may I be of service? My name is Henrietta."

Chapter 17

Silver Shines, Woodpeckers Chatter and Tap

"Does he know? Have you told him, Sebastian?" snapped Henrietta.

"Yes, your ladyship," Sebastian said with a small grin and a wink to Thomas.

"Mr. Sebastian Shrew," she snapped in a very deep and slow tone, "I would appreciate it if you would call me by my name and not some fictional title you have made up. Do we have an understanding?"

"Yes, yes," Sebastian said, smiling and once again winking at Thomas, "of course, your ladyship."

"My word, I give up!" Henrietta gasped. "Let's now find the box and give young Thomas the contents."

"Box? What box?" asked Thomas, looking directly toward the huge heron and the small shrew.

Sebastian again bowed his head toward Thomas, and in a hushed voice said, "I found a very special object in the hand of your mother, and after speaking to her ladyship, I am sure it was meant for you. I hid it in my wooden trinket box. I hid it safely, but my memory isn't what it used to be, you see, and now I can't find it and don't know where to look." Sebastian's voice was mournful.

Henrietta reassured him, "You did well, as you always do, Sebastian, even when you are fishing on my river. We will find it and return it to its rightful owner."

"What is in the box, Sebastian?" inquired Thomas.

As Sebastian was about to speak, Henrietta quickly interrupted. "In the box there is a whistle, a very special silver whistle. It has an engraving just for you, Thomas." She continued, "It is engraved 'T. Tobler,' and below your name is a very important message that I think you already know."

Thomas looked up at Henrietta and smiled. "It says," she began, *"Be pure of heart and true of word; friends will always be close by."* Thomas nodded and felt very proud. He believed he had learned those important values and had shown them on many occasions.

"First of all, we need to find where I hid it," said Sebastian. "Give me a moment." He sniffed the air. "I can smell that it is buried near an old walnut tree.

Thomas smiled. He loved the taste of his aunty's favorite recipe, worm-and-walnut cake. He turned and started to sniff at the ground, seeking that very special aroma.

"What on earth are you doing, Thomas?" squawked Henrietta. Thomas didn't reply but started sniffing farther away from his companions. Henrietta was now groaning, as she was becoming even more baffled watching the little mole scurrying about at great speed with his face seemingly buried in the soil.

Thomas then stopped abruptly and stood up. His face by now was completely black, covered in mud. He pointed and said, smiling proudly, "Just over there you will find the walnut tree. Walnuts are delicious with worms and rotten berries baked in a cake."

"Disgusting," said Henrietta.

"Not my cup of tea, but his nose is remarkable—spot on," said Sebastian.

The walnut tree drooped down, heavy with the green pods that contained the delicious nuts.

"My turn," said Henrietta. "I will use my skills to locate the box." She lifted her long neck high into the air and then threw it forward at great speed. She drove her long, sharp beak deeply into the soil close to the tree. "Nothing," she said as she continued to drive her beak into the ground. For what seemed to be hours, Henrietta continued to search, and every time she replied, "Nothing."

The next time, Henrietta threw her head back ever farther, and her beak pierced the soil. This time they all heard the sound they had been waiting for, the sound of her beak hitting a wooden object, one that wasn't solid. "Oh my, oh my," she gasped, "I think it's right down there."

Sebastian and Thomas now burrowed into the soil and made a tapping noise on the object. "Yes, this is it!" they shouted excitedly. They began to dig faster until they could lift the box out onto ground.

They all held their breath as Thomas stepped forward and slowly opened the lid of the box, which was wonderfully carved with creatures of the forest. The box was delicately lined with a soft, deep blue silk. As Thomas unfolded the silk, a bright light made him gasp. He looked down on the bright-silver whistle. Thomas shouted to Henrietta and Sebastian, "You were right, but I could never imagine it would be this beautiful."

There was a chain attached to the whistle, and Thomas placed it around his neck and held the whistle close to his heart. "I will treasure it forever and try my best every day."

Sebastian and Henrietta nodded and smiled. "Keep it secret and safe at all times, Thomas. When you need your friends, blow hard on the whistle," Sebastian instructed him.

"Now we must hurry—we must seek the help of two creatures who know the way through the woods to Hillfoot House," Henrietta said with some urgency.

"Oh, not those two woodpeckers! I always hear them in the trees complaining and moaning about everything. I have never even caught a glimpse of them. I don't trust any creature that I can't look in the eye," complained Sebastian.

"That's all well and good, Sebastian, and I agree that they are very peculiar and shy, but nevertheless we need them to help guide Thomas," reasoned Henrietta.

The three companions stared down at the map, and Sebastian pointed to Woodpecker Wood, not far from where they were. Hillfoot House was located on the other side of the wood, and Sebastian and Henrietta were sure that the woodpeckers could guide Thomas.

On the journey to Woodpecker Wood, Henrietta and Sebastian told Thomas as much as they could about the two woodpeckers, Penelope and Percival. Although they had never seen them close up, they could always hear them in the trees. Penelope was a very demanding wife to Percival. She had always wanted the perfect high-rise residence, situated in only the most desirable of ever-green trees. She was always heard shouting at Percival, whom she referred to as "Percy Dear." "The entrance hole is too small," she would say, or "The entrance hole is too big" or "That simply won't do, not good enough, Percy Dear. What would the neighbors think?"

Every day Penelope would list all of the reasons that Percival had failed miserably at his attempts to find a suitable residence. The quality of his workmanship and his eye for detail were simply not up to Penelope's exacting standards. Thomas and Henrietta chuckled as Sebastian quickly remarked, "I think you might say that poor old Percy Dear is seriously henpecked."

At the edge of the forest, they stopped and listened for any noise but heard nothing. The sun was now drawing in and they were discussing where to camp for the night when Sebastian cried out, "Shoosh. Listen!"

They could hear a series of taps and then voices in the distance, high in the trees. Henrietta shouted, "Percival, Penelope! Help us!"

As they all stood very still, looking high into the trees, two black objects were seen flying at great speed in between the branches. The birds would land on one tree and peck incredibly fast at the trunk for a few moments; then they would fly off again and repeat this on the next tree. "Percy Dear, again, this is simply not good enough—the wood is far too hard. How I will ever make a nest in these trunks?" a shrill voice said.

"We can help you find your perfect home if you help us in return!" Henrietta shouted.

The pecking stopped suddenly. "We are listening!" two voices chorused.

"Greedy, they are so very greedy, and not to be trusted!" Sebastian exclaimed, looking all around for the woodpeckers without success.

"Sebastian, please allow me to do the negotiating," said Henrietta.

Sebastian said nothing; he just sighed and nodded.

"We seek a safe path through your woods for our friend Thomas Tobler," Henrietta said, addressing the woodpeckers. "He needs to find Hillfoot House. In return, I offer my help as a guide to a wonderful forest far from here, where you will find your dream residence." Henrietta winked at Sebastian and Thomas, and then they waited for a reply.

"Well, Percy Dear, if you cannot provide the perfect home for us, I will happily take any offer of help. You have been trying for years and always fail, poor, poor, dear Percy," moaned Penelope. "Agreed!" she shouted down from high in the tress. "We will watch the mole from above. Keep heading east. If you hear one tap on the tree in front of you, stop and check your map, as you are moving off course. If you hear two taps on the tree ahead, it means you are following the correct path. When you here three or more, Hillfoot House will be close," Penelope instructed. "We leave at sunset. Be quick!" she shouted.

Sebastian was listening intently, and he shook his head. "Your ladyship, we cannot trust them. They are only interested in themselves…selfish creatures…untrustworthy. It is a trap, for sure."

Henrietta stretched her long wings around both Sebastian and Thomas and whispered, "They may be selfish, but I think their greed will make sure that they help guide Thomas."

Sebastian looked unusually tense, and replied in a less-than-confident tone, "If your wise and graceful ladyship is happy to let them guide Thomas, then I am happy."

Thomas, Sebastian, and Henrietta sat down and enjoyed a meal together. They were particularly impressed with the wonderful food that Aunty Edwina had prepared; the pickled fish was very quickly eaten by both Henrietta and Sebastian.

The sun was now passing behind the trees, and an impatient *tap, tap, tap* was heard high above in the tree canopy. "It is time… time for your journey to meet with Julius at Hillfoot House," announced Henrietta. Once again her long wings spread out, and Sebastian and Thomas moved close to her. "We are always here for you. Stay strong and true, and never forget who you are," she whispered softly to Thomas. "If you need us or any of your friends, you know what to do." She pointed to the whistle around Thomas's neck.

Thomas packed his rucksack, placed his walking stick under his paw, and slowly made his way eastward, looking back and waving and trying to smile confidently. Henrietta and Sebastian smiled and waved back as he passed the first few trees. He moved slowly forward, listening to the familiar *tap, tap* sound from above. Thomas was sure he was on the right path, the path he was to follow to finally meet Uncle Julius.

The forest became darker and darker as he traveled deeper and deeper into it. Thomas was making very good progress, regularly checking the map and listening for the taps. After some time he started to get confused. The taps were becoming less and less frequent, and soon he was hearing only one tap, which meant he was straying off course.

He stopped, worriedly checking the map over and over again. He stared down, studying it. Suddenly the wind started to gain strength and blew the map out of his paws and out of sight. Then, an icy cold rain started to fall as hard as ever, soaking him to his fur. He started to shiver. Then, as he listened, he heard no taps, no noises of the night—just the sound of the frightening weather and the darkness. Thomas spun around and looked into the distance, but he saw nothing.

"Maybe Sebastian was right. Maybe it is a trap, or something has gone terribly wrong," Thomas whispered to himself. Suddenly, he saw some black shapes moving out from behind the trees ahead. They were big creatures, and their footsteps were heavy. The ground began shaking as they ran toward him.

A bright light shone straight into his eyes. He couldn't see a thing. "It's him! Get him, lads!" Thomas heard a loud voice shouting.

Whack, whack! Something from behind hit him in the back of his head. Thomas looked up. The tunnel of bright light suddenly grew dim, and his breathing became heavy. In an instant his knees gave way, and he collapsed to the ground. Then darkness.

Chapter 18

Betrayed and Imprisoned

The light began to return as Thomas moved his head—which ached badly—forward. He couldn't see anything; he felt for his glasses, but they were nowhere near where he was lying. His whole body felt numb as his head moved from side to side so he could see where he was. From the blurred shapes, it looked as though he was in a small room with a door at one end. The door seemed very large, with what seemed to be bars running down a small window. Through the window he could just make out a dim, flickering light.

He used his other senses. Sniffing the air, it smelled very damp and musty, very much like a mole tunnel that hadn't be well tended to. As he sat up he felt extremely dizzy and decided to lie back down and take a few deep breaths. He started to move slowly around the room, feeling it out with his paws.

"No rucksack," he whispered, his heart skipping a beat as he felt his neck. Panicking, he started shouting, "My whistle, my beautiful whistle is gone."

He began to feel extremely frightened. To make things even worse, he began to hear footsteps coming toward the door. The footsteps were very slow and very heavy. Thomas lay down flat on the ground and held his breath as he looked up at the fuzzy outline of the window. He saw the outline of a large, round face appear and heard the jangling of keys opening a lock.

The creature pushed open the door. Thomas then saw an enormous figure standing over him with its head and shoulders bowed low. Its breath was deep and slow. Thomas could feel its warmth on his face. Thomas couldn't hold his breath any longer, and he gasped for air. The creature came closer to Thomas, and its giant paw moved from behind its back, heading directly toward Thomas's face.

Thomas closed his eyes, waiting for another blow to his head. However, he then heard a soft, calming voice say, "You may need these."

Thomas's eyes opened, and right in front of his eyes, the huge paw held out his glasses.

Thomas went to say something, but suddenly the paw covered his mouth.

"Be very quiet. If the master hears you and knows that I am talking to you, I will be punished," the creature said.

Thomas nodded his head, put on his glasses, and stared up at the mighty creature. It was a badger. It had very dark fur, with white stripes on its face and deep, dark eyes that gazed down at Thomas intently. "My name is Dachs, and you are being held here on suspicion of spying."

"But I am the nephew of Julius—my name is Thomas Tobler. Can you tell him I am here? I am sure there has been a misunderstanding," Thomas pleaded.

"I don't know about that. The master tells us we must capture anyone close to Hillfoot House, as he likes his privacy, and you were on his property, his private property," explained Dachs.

Thomas wanted to tell the badger his story, but again the large paw covered his mouth. "You will be able to talk to the master soon. He is just deciding what to do with some other intruders me and the lads captured tonight," Dachs said with a contented grin.

Thomas was feeling scared, but again he thought back to the general and all of his stories of captures and escapes. He decided to stay silent, nod, and think of a plan. Suddenly, they heard another voice. Thomas looked at Dachs, and the badger suddenly went very tense. As they both listened, the voice began to scream.

"DACHS, DACHS, bring me the last criminal! I am tired and wish to pass sentence. Hurry, hurry, servant!" the voice echoed.

"Yes, Master, at once," replied Dachs as he moved closer to Thomas and whispered in his ear. "If you want to get out of here and back to wherever you came from, just agree with whatever the master says. Don't—whatever you do—challenge him on anything."

Thomas said nothing but stood up as tall as he could and slowly walked behind the imposing badger toward the door. As the door opened, Thomas saw a long pathway. The walls and floor were made of gray cobblestones, and it was cold—icy cold.

The voice started to scream again, "DACHS, DACHS! Where are you, you useless, lumbering fellow?"

"Master, I am on my way! I have the last one for you. I think he is injured," Dachs responded in a very hushed voice.

"Think? Think? I don't pay you to think! Be quick, servant, it is late and I need food!" bellowed the strange voice.

"Hurry, hurry, little mole, the master is getting angry," Dachs urged, pushing Thomas toward the end of the walkway, where he could see an enormous, dark, oak door with a huge, golden handle. There was also a brass plaque, which read:

You have entered the grounds of Hillfoot House illegally. Now face your punishment.

It was signed "Master Julius."

Thomas stood very still and silent. Was this his Uncle Julius? Could it be that he was to face his own relative, who meant to harm him? Thomas stood as upright as he could, with his chest pushed out, and shook the paw of the giant badger. He shouted as loud as he could, "Dachs, please inform Uncle Julius that his nephew and rightful owner of Hillfoot House is here and will see him now." He looked up at Dachs, smiled, and winked.

"Ah yes, yes, Mr. Thomas, thank you, yes sir."

As the large, golden handle was pushed down, the mighty, oak door opened. It opened into a magnificent hall with brightly colored walls and flooring. Huge pots with what seemed to be jewelry lay all about, and at the back of the hall was a huge throne. On the throne sat a very large mole covered from head to paw in gold and silver jewelry. On the top of the throne sat two jet-black birds with deep-red eyes who were making loud tapping noises on the side of the throne.

The mole opened up his hand and started to wave a silver chain around and around in circles, laughing. "Oh, I know who you are, Thomas Tobler. My faithful servants here have led you to me," he sneered, pointing at the two birds. "DACHS, DACHS, bring him before me!" he shouted again.

The badger went to usher Thomas forward toward Julius. As he did, Thomas calmly placed his paw on Dachs's paw, looked up at his face, and said, "That will be all…thank you, Dachs, please leave us."

"Yes sir, certainly sir," Dachs said, turning back toward the door. He smiled back at Thomas and gently closed it.

"DACHS, DACHS, come back, you fool!" Julius snapped angrily. The two birds started tapping excitedly as Julius started to rant and rave.

Thomas stood right in front of his uncle and said very politely, "Hello, Uncle. I have come to claim my inheritance. Shall we talk?"

The two woodpeckers started to flap their wings. Julius, waving his paws in the air in a rage, said, "Be gone, servants. Leave me and the boy alone."

The larger of the two birds passed to Julius what seemed to be a piece of folded paper, and the smaller bird squawked, "Let's go, Percy Dear, our job is done for the master." They flew right past Thomas, squawking, "Tap, tap, tap, tap" and staring right into his eyes.

Julius started to calm down and signalled for Thomas to join him on his elegant throne. Thomas felt uneasy as his uncle's paw reached out and drew him close. "My boy," Julius began, "I know who you are, and I have read the writing on your map. Indeed, it says that you are the rightful owner of Hillfoot House. I also have found a gift especially for me from my dear Edwina and Albert," he continued with a sarcastic tone. "First, let me tell you what I think of the writing on the map." Julius started to get angry again and pulled Thomas toward him as he tore up the map that Thomas valued so much. Thomas pushed away from Julius as his uncle started screaming at the top of his voice, "That is what I think of that! Oh, and let me read you this letter from your aunt and uncle," he sneered.

From the edge of his throne he took a small letter out of the box that Thomas had been carrying in his rucksack. He started to read it.

Julius, you have taken so much from our family, and without reason. This makes us very sad. Hillfoot House is not yours, and we object to you taking it and using it to steal and plunder from all of the folk living nearby. You use easily corrupted creatures to carry out your evil work.

Thomas is honest and true to the Tobler family values. You can no longer stay here and must hand over all of your possession to Thomas immediately, so that he can do the rightful thing.

Julius again reached out for his nephew, but this time Thomas pushed him away. Julius flew into another rage, this time tearing the letter to pieces. He looked directly at Thomas, his mouth open and covered in saliva, as he began to pant and screech breathlessly. "That's what I think of you and the Tobler family. This house is mine, all the treasure is mine, and you are mine."

Thomas leaped forward, pushing his uncle back and grabbing the whistle and chain. He jumped off of the throne and started to move as quickly as he could toward the door.

Julius screamed, "Servants, servants! Come now!"

Thomas stopped at the door and looked at the whistle, remembering the words that were engraved on it. As he was about to blow the whistle, the door flew open, and two more mighty badgers grabbed him under both paws and dragged him toward Julius. These two

badgers were young and strong, and Thomas couldn't shake himself from their grip. One of them ripped the whistle from Thomas's grasp. He bowed at Julius and said, "Master, here is what you desire."

Julius, weighed down by all of his jewelry, slid off the throne stood in front of Thomas. He blew the whistle. He blew and blew, but no sound came from it.

He started to shout and scream. "It's a trick! This is just a useless trinket—nobody will come to your aid, no friends are close!" He threw the whistle to the floor and pressed his face into Thomas's. "Friends, friends." He scowled. "I have no friends. I don't want any friends, and I just need my servants." He started to laugh as he looked straight at Thomas.

Thomas looked straight into his uncle's eyes and said calmly, "You have my pity."

Julius was so enraged he could hardly breathe, and for a moment he stood back and looked at Thomas as he drew some long, deep breaths. "Sadly, I have to pass a sentence on what many would consider one of my own, but a criminal is a criminal. Tonight you will be taken away from here, and in the morning you will face your punishment. Be gone."

Again Thomas remained calm and stared at his uncle, remembering the general's wise words: "When faced with an enemy that uses anger and violence, always respond with calmness and intelligence, dear boy."

Julius shouted again, "Put this repulsive creature into the lower dungeon and wake me in the morning. His punishment will be witnessed by all."

As Thomas was dragged away, Dachs rushed past and started to try and reason with Julius. "Master, please Master, I think you may need to think about this after a good night's sleep. Please, Master, let me prepare you a nice meal. The lower dungeons are very prone to flooding, Master."

Julius paused and whispered, "A meal is fine idea, yes, servant, that would be agreeable. Make it quickly and clean all of this mess in my throne room." He continued to whisper, "I told you, Dachs, you are not paid to think, and if you question me again, you will be punished—like the last time."

Dachs bowed low and said solemnly, "Yes, master. At once, master. Understood, master."

Julius pushed Dachs aside and shouted at the two other badgers who were holding Thomas, "Take him away."

Thomas looked back at his uncle and shook his head. He looked at Dachs and smiled as he was dragged out of the hall and down the walkway.

On and on the walkway went. Thomas's arms were being squeezed tightly. Then, finally, they reached another door that was locked. Thomas was thrown down while one of the badgers unlocked the door. The second one pointed and said, "Get in, criminal, and think of your crime and your inevitable punishment. Tomorrow the master will make an example of you."

"Come on," the first badger said, "we have to make everything secure. The great storm is coming." They laughed as the key turned with a huge clunking sound. They slowly walked away.

Thomas was now in danger, very grave danger.

Chapter 19

History Repeating Itself—an Adventure in Vain?

The storm had been raging for days, but it seemed that tonight it was going to be at its most violent. Thomas knew that the river was close to bursting its banks, and that the area around Hillfoot House was notorious for flooding. He was hoping that Julius had spent some of his vast riches on flood defenses.

From inside the small, cell-like room, Thomas could hear the wind howling outside and the branches of nearby trees snapping and falling to the ground. He decided to move around the room on his knees, feeling as he went, to see if there was any way of escape. The floor was very cold and damp, and in places, small puddles of water had gathered. It was fresh water, and that was a concern.

He decided to feel the inner walls, and again the dampness gave way to areas of leaking water—not great, gushing amounts, but trickles of icy cold water. Cupping his paws together, he gathered some of the water that was leaking from the walls and took a series of long sniffs, in and out, in and out. "Oh my, this water is coming directly from the river. I don't have much time!" he exclaimed.

The only thing he could do was to dig directly down close by the door, trying to tunnel his way into the corridor and then attempting to escape Hillfoot House. As he started to dig, Thomas realized that the soil was a very dense clay, and as hard as he dug, he wasn't making great progress. But his determination and self-belief pushed him to dig harder and harder. The clay soil was starting to move, but very slowly.

He stopped and listened. His heart was pumping hard, and he was breathing deeply. He could just make out the faint sound of gushing water beyond the walls of the room. He dug even harder and more quickly; he was beneath the door frame when his paws started to feel very wet. Water was now flooding up from underneath where he was burrowing, and the trickles coming from the walls were now becoming a series of waterspouts.

He could hear muffled voices coming from along the walkways and passages outside, and he noticed lots of flickering lights. It was now becoming very clear to Thomas that there was no escape; he was just waiting for the floodwater to break through the walls and wash him away. He moved to where the floor was drier and held his head in his hands.

"Dearest Mother and Father, I have journeyed a long way seeking the truth and have found it. I am happy that I know who I am, and I have tried my best to live up to the Tobler family values." He started to weep. "I don't want to die not like this, not like them."

He heard a soft croaking sound coming from the ceiling, and then the flapping of wings. Then he sensed the movement of something coming toward him. A small, dark-colored bird had landed and perched itself on his shoulder. Nose to beak, they looked straight at each other, straining to see in the dim light.

"It is sad, the story you tell," the small bird said. "I, too, was on a journey to find my parents, who had disappeared when I was led here by two woodpeckers who told me they knew where to find them."

"They fooled me, too, and now I am alone, just like you," Thomas said mournfully.

"My name is Bran, and I am a raven." The small bird held out his wing tip and touched Thomas's shoulder affectionately.

"Bran, it is a very great shame that we have to meet like this. Is there any way out?" asked Thomas.

"The only way I see is to make as much noise as we can and hope and pray that someone hears us, but the storm floods are coming, and I don't hold out much hope," said Bran.

The young mole and the even younger raven sat together, looked up at the ceiling. They began to shout. "Help us, anyone help us! We are down here! Help!"

All they could hear was the sound of the water starting to gush up through the floor and walls. By now the water was covering Thomas's feet, and his paws were starting to feel numb with the cold.

"Wait. I will fly to the ceiling and try and to peck our way out," said Bran.

Thomas smiled, but in his heart, he knew it was just a matter of time until the waters came crashing in.

Bran pecked harder and harder on the ceiling above. For such a small creature, he seemed to be very strong. Soil started to fall from where he was pecking. He continued as Thomas shouted for help. The water was now knee deep, and the walls were starting to make loud creaking noises. Bran was exhausted, and he glided back to Thomas's shoulder, his head bowed low in defeat.

By now Thomas was feeling sleepy and dazed. "Stay awake, Thomas, don't drift off," squawked Bran. Just then, a huge crack appeared in one of the walls, and the water started to gush in. Thomas began to feel completely numb from his waist down and began to slip down onto his knees.

Bran flew at great speed up to the ceiling, pecking with all of his might. He looked down at his poor, helpless friend, and tears fell down his cheeks. He was sure that this was the end. By now he had no strength to peck anymore and was about to fly down to see if he could help Thomas, when he heard a loud, thudding noise coming from directly above.

One thud, and then another, and one more. A long, white beak appeared like a dagger through the ceiling, and a small pinprick of light shone through. Bran started to peck and squawk excitedly. He looked down at Thomas, who was slumped on his side with water slowly lapping over his body. He was so still, making no sound.

The pinprick became a small hole and then a larger hole. Bran could now clearly hear many different voices. He was startled when the very distinct head of a heron poked through the hole. "Where is the mole? Where is Thomas?" she squawked.

"Down there, on the floor in the water. Please hurry!" Bran said anxiously.

"Well done, young raven. I am Henrietta, and I have many friends here to help. Now stand aside!"

Squawking anxiously, Bran flew through the hole into the night air. As he looked down, he saw the most amazing sight: a small gathering of creatures busily chattering away and exchanging instructions. It looked as though a rescue party had arrived. Bran hoped it wasn't too late.

Chapter 20

New and Old Friends to the Rescue

"Tallyho, I see the poor little chap, and it looks like he is still breathing," boomed the general. "Corporal Francis, prepare the emergency first aid, blankets, and warm clothes on standby," he continued, barking his orders.

"Yes sir, at once, General," Frankie responded instantly, saluting at the same time.

"Skipper, I say Skipper, is the escape craft all prepared and ready?" the general inquired.

"The good boat *Carpe Diem* is as ready as she will ever be, General, but I am not sure how long these moorings can hold, sir," shouted Sebastian as loudly as he could.

The wind roared, trees were being flattened, and all around, the crumbled remains of Hillfoot House were being washed away into the darkness.

"Bats, bats—call the Brotherhood of Bats!" shrieked the general, waving and pointing into the hole and down into the room where Thomas lay.

Frankie the field mouse, or Corporal Francis, as he was known during tactical operations, repeatedly shouted all of the general's orders, using his homemade bullhorn.

Before long, the flapping of wings and the loud chatter of voices all speaking at the same time could be heard in the distance. The general looked up into the night sky. Large black shapes with orange eyes began to form into one huge, dark object which then started screeching excitedly.

The final order was given. "Down here! Your brother is in need of you help—hurry!" The general, Henrietta, and Corporal Francis stood over the entrance of the hole and pointed the way. The Brotherhood flew higher and higher into the night sky, their wings now flapping as one, drowning out the sound of the wind and water.

Boom, boom, boom! The black shape sped down toward the rescue party. The bats, with the magnificent Boris at the front as usual, flew straight down through the entrance and deep into the underground room.

"I say, chaps, credit where credit is due. I have never said it before, but those fly-boys put on a darn good show!" The general smiled and saluted in the direction from which the Brotherhood had flown.

"General, your ladyship, we have only got moments. I have to cast off or we will not make it. Hurry as fast as you can," screamed Sebastian.

"Right you are, Skipper. Corporal Francis, let us make our way to the boat. Henrietta, my dear, please direct the bats to the boat and join us as soon as you can," the general ordered. He had the situation under contro, and, as usual, was very calm.

Henrietta once again peered into the hole. All she could see were the dark shapes of the bats clambering around a motionless Thomas. Bran soon flew down by her side.

"Will he be OK?" he asked. "I haven't know him long, but he is very brave."

"I don't know, young raven, I hope so. Thomas is a fine young mole."

Loud screeches were now coming from below. "We have him! We have our brother mole, and he is alive! Fly, brothers, fly!" The booming started again, and the dark object began to rise up from the room. As they rose, all that could be heard was the deafening crash of all four walls giving in to the huge pressure of the river.

Henrietta and Bran held their breath and waited. A huge blast of warm air and the incredible booming of hundreds of bat wings passed them in a flash. "Let's go! You want to be with you new friend, if I am not mistaken?" she said to the young raven.

"That would be wonderful!" screeched Bran.

The two birds flew as low and as fast as they could, trying to keep up with the brotherhood. As they looked down, they saw a few figures holding lamps, the lights running in all directions as they tried to find a safe route away from the floodwaters. The lights soon went out, and the figures disappeared, taken away by the river. It had nearly immersed all of Hillfoot House by now. Only a few small outbuildings remained standing; the surrounding woodland was flattened and completely submerged.

The *Carpe Diem* was being thrown up and down and from side to side as the rescue party started to arrive. "Everyone safe and on board? Ready to cast off?" shouted the skipper. There was lots of noise as the last of the bats lowered Thomas onto the boat.

"Moorings ready for release, Skipper," said the general with a salute. His sharp quills sliced the ropes, and the *Carpe Diem* rose up and onto the fast-moving water. The skipper, ably assisted by Frankie, took charge of directing the boat along the gushing river.

Everyone else had only one concern: Thomas, who was now covered in warming blankets. His body was cold, and he was breathing very slowly.

Boris stepped forward, shaking his head. "His small body is frozen, and I am afraid it may be too late for our brother."

Everyone in the boat bowed their heads. Boris picked Thomas up and drew him close to his huge chest. "Brotherhood, he needs your warmth," cried Boris. He wrapped his giant wings tightly around Thomas's body. All of the other bats joined wings and wrapped themselves around their leader. The crew of friends stood in silence, watching and praying that this may somehow help Thomas.

After what seemed a long time, strange shapes started to appear against the skin of the bats. "Our brother is saved!" shrieked Boris as the layers of dark wings unfolded and a very weak, but very alive, Thomas managed a small smile. He was gently helped to the relative warmth of the skipper's cabin. It was now time for him to eat a little and rest.

Calmer water was ahead, and the first glimpse of a new day started to brighten the dark, stormy sky. Boris stepped forward, lowered one wing to the deck of the boat, and bowed to all of the friends on board. "My special friends," he said, "it was our honor to help you and our brother. If at any time you need the brotherhood, just call."

The general stood to attention, and looked over at Corporal Francis, who quickly followed suit, standing up smartly. Henrietta, Bran, and the skipper saluted and waved as the brotherhood started to slowly rise off of the deck and high into the air.

One final, huge shout blasted into the air: "Brotherhood, fly!" The bats then rose at great speed high into the sky and disappeared in what seemed a second.

As the sun began to rise, the clouds started to disappear, and a warm, sweet breeze began to blow. Thomas, now able to stand, started talking to all of his friends. "How did you know where we were?" he said, looking at Henrietta

The skipper interrupted, "Someone told us what had happened to you, and he had the good sense to raise the alarm and blow the whistle. You might know him as Dachs, and he is waiting for us when we get back to safer shores."

Henrietta continued, "It seems that when the whistle is blown by someone of true heart, their close friends will hear it and know that they are in danger. So, it seems that this badger has a good heart, Thomas."

Thomas smiled and nodded, "Yes, he does. I knew it. I just knew it."

Henrietta pointed toward the small raven. "If it wasn't for all of the squawking and pecking noises coming from this young bird, we might have been too late."

Bran flew onto Thomas's shoulder, squawked, and said, "That's what any creature would do for a friend."

The sun rose higher, and a welcome, clear blue, morning sky appeared. The air was warm, and the sounds of all of the woodland creatures returned. The skipper had navigated the small boat onto familiar waters, and soon they saw the riverbank where he loved to fish. They could see a large shape on the edge of the riverbank. "It's Dachs!" shouted Thomas. The badger started to wave.

All of the friends got off the boat as the skipper tied it up to his mooring stumps. "Master, you are safe, Master!" Dachs said humbly, kneeling and bowing before Thomas.

"My dear Dachs, I am not your master," Thomas whispered.

"But you are the true owner of Hillfoot House, and therefore I am you servant, Master," replied the large badger.

"There is little left of Hillfoot House, and Julius has gone, washed away by the floods. There is nothing left for me there. I want to go back to my real home now," Thomas said quietly. "Be free and roam wild, faithful Dachs. Your act of bravery and loyalty saved me."

Dachs reached out and placed the chain and the silver whistle around Thomas's neck. He embraced Thomas and held him tightly, whispering, "I can never thank you enough. You have freed me."

Thomas stood tall at the edge of the riverbank and addressed all of his friends. "I have come a long way and have learned so many important things from such special family and friends. I would like you all to come with me for shelter, warmth, and many good meals at the home of my aunty and uncle."

The friends cheered, squawked, and boomed, and they even heard a friendly croak saying, *"Qui, qui, mes amis."*

Thomas and his group of very close friends made the short journey to Albert and Edwina's inviting home. As he excitedly knocked on their door, Thomas was met with the most delicious smells. Suddenly, all of the friends felt very hungry.

Edwina opened the door and immediately burst into floods of tears. Albert squeezed Thomas tightly and said softly, "Welcome home, Thomas Tobler."

All of the friends, Thomas, and his aunty and uncle enjoyed many days of wonderful parties to celebrate Thomas's homecoming. Soon, Thomas was having another rucksack packed full of food for his final journey—back to his home in Endingen. This time he wouldn't be alone; his friends would show him the way and accompany him for most of the journey. Also, one new, but very close, friend would be coming to stay with him. Bran and Thomas were by now inseparable.

They soon arrived at the edge of the forest he had left a long time ago. Thomas made his very emotional farewells to family and friends, who would now be regular visitors.

"Simply splendid serving alongside you, my boy. You shall take the honorary rank of sergeant," the general began.

"But, but—" said Frankie.

"Corporal Francis, don't interrupt!" barked the general.

"Thank you, General and Frankie, we had many scrapes and always did quite well." Thomas chuckled. He turned to the others. "Henrietta, Sebastian, and Tobias—such wise and wonderful friends. Without your guidance, I wouldn't be here today."

"A pleasure, my dear Thomas. Please come and spend some time on my river," Henrietta said.

"And in my good vessel," squeaked Sebastian.

"And on my lake," croaked Tobias.

There was no need for words as Thomas embraced Uncle Albert and Aunt Edwina. They knew that their family bond was strong, and that they would see each other soon.

Thomas and Bran waved as they disappeared over a small bank and dug down into Thomas's tunnel. Thomas felt very content and safe. With Bran, he now had a friend, companion, and kindred spirit. "Well, here we are. Time to relax—no more adventures," Thomas said, laughing.

"To new beginnings," squawked Bran.

Thomas sat in his comfortable old leather chair, and Bran perched on his shoulder. Thomas looked over at his small wooden table and noticed a large white envelope. He opened it, took out a letter, paused for a moment, and then read aloud.

My Dearest Thomas,

While you were seeking Hillfoot House, I paid a visit to your aunty and uncle. I thought that all of your family should know that when I found your parents on that very sad day, I also found your silver whistle. What you don't know is that I found another, identical whistle. I hadn't the heart to burden you or your family with any more sad news at the time. So I have enclosed the other whistle. I hope and pray it brings you joy, and not heartbreak.

Your very close friend,
Sebastian Shrew

Thomas smiled and reached into the bottom of the envelope. He held the silver whistle and chain in his left paw and looked at the engraving. It read:

A. Tobler
Be strong and stand tall. Family will walk the same path.

Thomas squeezed both of the whistles tightly in his paws and held them close to his heart. His whole body trembled. Bran flew around the room, squawking excitedly.

"It is the greatest day of my life...I have a brother or sister!" shrieked Thomas. "I have a brother or sister!"